Aakash is an International Development consultant with a decade of experience in social research and public policy. His work focused on leveraging technology to extend financial services to rural and low-income households in Asia and Africa. Additionally, he runs a travel blog, handofcolors.me, which has garnered recognition among the country's leading travel blogs. Constantly traversing the globe for work, he seeks to discover the human moments in travel, immerse himself in diverse cultures, and absorb the profound philosophies embedded in each. His first novel, *The Other Guy,* was published in 2018. *Out of My Oyster* is his second novel.

Out of My Oyster

AAKASH MEHROTRA

Om FIGMENT
An Imprint of Om Books International

First published in 2026 by

Om FIGMENT An Imprint of **Om Books International**

Corporate & Editorial Office
A-12, Sector 64, Noida 201 301
Uttar Pradesh, India
Phone: +91 120 477 4100
Email: editorial@ombooks.com
Website: www.ombooksinternational.com

Sales Office
107, Ansari Road, Darya Ganj,
New Delhi 110 002, India
Phone: +91 11 4000 9000
Fax: +91 11 2327 8091
Email: sales@ombooks.com
Website: www.ombooks.com

ISBN: 978-93-6395-861-6

Printed in India

10 9 8 7 6 5 4 3 2 1

This book is dedicated to every queer individual I have interacted with, and in the process, I have discovered myself. To the voices that refuse to be silenced, to the stories that demand to be told. To the allies who listen, advocate, and stand in solidarity, creating spaces where acceptance is not conditional but inherent. And to the generations to come, may they inherit a world where identity is not debated but simply lived.

This is for you.

Contents

And That Changed Everything

It was slowly becoming clear in the office; Atulya, our old corporate strategy lead, was leaving. Even when I heard the words, they didn't fully register. I just stared at him, expressionless, trying to process it. Some people leave a mark so deep that letting go feels personal, even if your day-to-day work didn't directly intersect with theirs. That's what Atulya was to many of us. He wasn't just another colleague in a different department—he was the steady, invisible force that made everything feel like it worked. His energy was infectious.

Although I was in the creative wing and rarely had to collaborate with him formally, his presence was always felt in meetings, brainstorming sessions, and even casual conversations. Atulya had built relationships, nurtured teams, and had a way of showing up—calm, insightful, and always listening. His energy was uplifting; he had this rare gift of being both a mentor and a peer, slipping effortlessly between roles. He was the heartbeat of the entire office, a person who could uncloak his professional attire and be your close associate or confidante in a jiffy. That's why his leaving felt like more than just a change in staffing. It felt like the soul of the place was shifting. I kept wondering whether anyone could truly fill the space he would leave behind.

Atulya appreciated and stood by me when I wanted to start a weekly show to bring out stories of queer people. He wanted our channel to take a progressive stand when the ruling on Section 377 started. The debate had to start before the judges penned down their judgment, and I wanted to put before the world the many untold stories that would go unmentioned, and through those stories initiate a wider debate in society.

Before India could tread on the liberal path, the society needed to know that another world existed, a little different from how they see theirs, but similar in the way they live. The world needed to know that there were numerous stories of discrimination, heartbreak, pain, and ecstasy hidden in some closets. These stories needed an audience. They needed closure, and a proper coming out. Taking such a step towards equality would have been a huge move for any radio station — but someone had to do it. And as Atulya said, "Give me a good reason to convince myself to not go for something as big and liberating as this."

He was leaving—soon to be replaced by a man in his early thirties, a polished alumnus of Carnegie University with the distinction of having steered one of the largest mergers in the advertising world. It wasn't hard to read between the lines. The board, perhaps spooked by a sea of red on the balance sheets, had chosen someone they believed could play the game of numbers better, someone whose instincts were sharper on the commercial front. It was a strategic move, no doubt, but it felt clinical, almost surgical. As if fixing the company required cutting out its heart.

The new guy was, quite simply, magnificent. There was no better word for it. Tall, composed, with an eye-catching physique. He was a striking contrast to Atulya's pudgy, middle-aged frame. It was the kind of change that made people sit up straighter, adjust their tone, and watch their reflection a little more closely in the glass walls of the office.

"Meet Anuj. That program I was telling you about. That was his idea," Atulya said, beaming at both of us.

I smiled a measured smile. Atulya had offered me creative liberty to run the program the way I wanted; commercial success wasn't our metric, it was long forlorn, and Atulya had taken that program as a social responsibility.

"It's nice to meet you, Anuj. I am Dhruv," he introduced himself, holding out his hand.

I took it after a second's hesitation and said, "It's a pleasure meeting you. I have heard quite a lot about you."

"I hope not the infamous things," his tone was formal and almost dismissive, even when he was trying to be casual.

"Well, if being called a nerdy corporate hot-shot counts as infamy, then yes—your reputation has preceded you." I could hear the words leave my mouth, light and clipped, but what unsettled me more was the smile that accompanied them. It settled on my face uninvited, awkwardly out of place, betraying more than I intended to show.

"I'm not sure," he replied, pausing just long enough to make it sound deliberate. "But for a first meeting, I'll take that as a compliment." Bummer. My little jab had been neatly deflected, smoothed over with corporate finesse. If it were a power play, I'd just been outmaneuvered with a smile.

There was this merest hint of a twinkle in his eyes. The lad in me wanted to chuckle, but the corporate guy in me abstained.

"That show has been nominated for an award this year," Atulya interrupted, and the little seemingly argument died in the smiles.

"And I am sure it'll win. Genuine things always do! And with a hand on my heart, I can say that I breathe in a sense of pride in joining a place that's always brought new ideas forth, and stood by seemingly unconventional but liberating ideas," he said hotly, looking at Atulya, with a great deal of reverence in his voice.

Atulya smiled; we all did.

"Well, as I see, I will be mostly occupied with the business team, but I do hope to catch up with the creative teams as much as possible. And believe me, my heart lies more with ideas than numbers," he smiled, with a remarkable warmth in his smile.

For a few moments, my mind lingered on the cool, composed way he had spoken to me. There was no pretence—just a quiet balance. He was authoritative when he needed to sound someone off with it, but just as easily slipped into warmth when addressing a room. There was a natural ease to him, a genial undercurrent that softened the sharp edges of his presence.

My mind went to analyze all the hearsay about how the channel has been losing audience, and the new guy has been brought in to turn around things, and that everything would get more business-oriented, and individuality, which was always coveted, would take a backseat. There was a tempest in my mind, and all I could respond with was a tired sigh. Suddenly I felt the urge to down a pint of beer, or maybe something stronger.

I nudged myself to take this break. I was drowning, and no one knew it. I put my laptop in sleep mode, took a copy of my script, and headed to have a pint.

I was just about to flag over the bartender for a fill when someone slid onto the stool on my right, and when I turned and caught a glimpse of the person, I nearly lost my breath. Gosh! It was Dhruv sitting next to me. He was gorgeous, and perhaps all I needed was some strong feeling to gauge his appeal. He was handsome in an understated way; the aquiline nose he sported complemented his prominent jaw bones. He looked flamboyant in character.

And he smiled, a perfectly balanced smile, the two curves tucking right in the middle of his cheeks, in some orderly manner, as if religiously rehearsed, and his entrancing, slow-shaped eyes lit with joy. I could imagine them resembling two pools of flashing fire. They shone brightly, like two sapphires, swimming with joy. I could imagine him to have a vivacious character quite different from the strong, pragmatic corporate guy he had been portrayed as. There was a fine judgment of balancc and proportion in his physique, and his corporate attire did its best to bring out his timeless handsomeness. There was almost a feminine prettiness to his appeal, evoking, kind of introverted depth, a longing of a dreamy quality.

And in his sonorous, rumbling voice, with a smile almost draped on his face, Dhruv said, "I saw you coming down to the bar. I was a little shy of heading here alone, and that too on the first day of office; but I believe with your company it wouldn't be much noticed," he said almost booming out a guffaw, but I found it a kind of mellifluous.

"You know the industry, anything and everything can make a noise. But don't worry, things usually go unnoticed here. Though your ruthless, turn-the-tables corporate guy image will take a hit after this," I replied with a humorous retort.

He looked down, smiled, and then looked at me, a deep, piercing gaze almost making me feel naked.

There was a smirk on his lips, "Ruthless, turn the table corporate guy… damn I had no idea these will be the words I'll be greeted with. I think I should hire an image consultant now!"

"Is that a part of corporate strategy?" I asked inquisitively.

I watched his sharp eyes float down the surface of my face, and then he raised a dark, perfectly arched brow and said, "Image building is always a part of strategy, isn't it?"

I nodded.

The beer glasses were before us, I raised it for a toast, and asked, "What's your beer taste?"

He looked taken by this abrupt question, "I stayed in Belgium for a year before my graduation, and I was only brewing and drinking beer that entire year. I am a certified beer taster and have even led groups on beer brewing tours. So I think I can easily say I have acquired a sophisticated taste for beer," he answered with a graceful smile on his face.

I was impressed.

"You should write this on your LinkedIn profile, this will do better than an image consultant," I could see a small, triumphant smile tilt up the edges of his lips.

I raised my beer glass again to say that I was impressed. He raised his, too, and gave another affectionate smile. I don't know if that was the honesty of that moment, and we were in it, or was it his perfectly placed, flirtatious smile, but I was drawn to him.

"Well, before I forget, I truly appreciate your show on queer voices, and I hope it's getting a good traction among listeners too. If I may suggest, you can make it more diverse, some love stories which do not fit in the perfect, heteronormative boxes as prevalent in our country," he said with an air of sagacity in his voice.

"You will have to explain this a bit more," a little confused, and equally eager to extend the conversation.

He took a breath, "Simple, why can't a story of a disabled couple fit here, or someone who broke boundaries of religion for their love, or a love story blossoming at old age, just more diversity. One colour may look good for some time, but to make it a pretty affair for perpetuity, you need a rainbow," he said, almost looking for my concurrence, as some kid.

"If I may be candid, a part of me says 'yes', and a part fears that the program will be diluted."

"Wasn't the idea of the show to chase love stories which are different from the way we see them, or have been shown? You are talking about diversity, and are reluctant to give it space in your program. I can get you are part of the community, so there is a propensity to remain within that spectrum, that's natural. But broadening the spectrum broadens your scope of creativity. But again, it's just a suggestion, no meddling in the way creative teams work, and it's your show, and it's your prerogative to see how you take it." The honesty in his eyes touched me.

"At a moment when so much of what becomes artistic canon is based within narrow traditions, it is intellectually and artistically rewarding to be part of a collection where the focus is on multiplicity. I can say, it's not a bad idea to expand the boundaries, we can talk more about it, and give it a try," I turned to face him a little, leaning an elbow to the bar, and letting his gaze pierce through my skin.

Something about the way he was looking at me made me flush with pleasure. Something about the brightness in his eyes, or the angle of his head, made me think he was an exceptional listener.

He shrugged, rotating on his stool so that his knees brushed against mine. My eyes met his, and there was a gleam of appreciation in his eyes. I felt at ease, and in that, I failed to realize that I was falling into the guilt trap.

I wanted to feel sane. I closed my eyes briefly after Dhruv left to meet Atulya. I tried to reflect on that half an hour spent with him that pushed me down the whirlpool. The suggestive tone, the wicked grin, the way he leaned forward to talk, stressing on certain words, and his eyes danced with mischief as he said those, the playful badinage between us, the way he rolled his eyes as he smiled, and his proximity at moments; everything had a potent effect on me. I wish those thirty minutes could be wiped from my memory, but moments like these would reshape my life.

***

I walked through the footpath, slowly stepping on dried leaves. The rustle as I stepped on them was oddly satisfying. I looked at them bemusedly, their golden hue of the lighter side stood out against the ambers and bronze of the sunbaked sand. I wished to reach down, pick them up, smooth the creases, and keep them as a collection of beautiful memories, but something told me to leave them to the footpath, where they belonged.

Just then, another golden leaf pirouetted down an invisible streak of breeze and blew past my face. It left me smiling. I ran my fingers through my hair, adjusted my spectacles, and looked down at the scattered, sun-bleached corpses of summer. Fallen leaves—once vibrant, now brittle—lying quietly in surrender. There was something oddly comforting in their decay. The tree, after all, remains. It greens, then sheds its leaves as they get old, and as it sheds, it regains its energy to grow new leaves for the next cycle. Isn't this old dying for a new lease of life, something elementary to the natural cycle? I looked up at the sky, and a smile crept onto my face. I could see a part of my life resonating with this natural cycle.

I halted at a French confectionery to get my daily dose of waffles. I chose to sit down and relish the waffles, and as I looked out, the wheezing traffic, passersby walking, and the gentle feeling of everything around slowing as the night crept and the old forms dying to give space to the new; my mind drifted, and thoughts of Dhruv occupied me. I felt defenceless and awkwardly embarrassed. I chuckled like a school-girl, but deep down the thoughts had to be killed.

I messaged Nikhil again—it was the third time that morning, following our usual polite exchange of good mornings and emojis that no longer carried real warmth. I was feeling desperate. They say absence makes the heart grow fonder; in my case, it was growing anxious, dependent, and quite resentful.

The distance between Nikhil and me was not limited to different geographies and flight schedules. It had stretched into something more abstract, more painful—an emotional chasm Nikhil was still the carefree soul of the college days—charming, impulsive, unfazed by consequence. And I had unwittingly bent myself into the shape of his world—curving around his moods, anchoring myself to his needs, adjusting silently to his version of love. It was stifling. I don't even remember when it stopped being mutual.

We lived in different dimensions. He lived in his playful youth, who now had the money to buy more happiness. There were shiny distractions—weekend parties, new sneakers, spontaneous getaways, selfies with colleagues. I wanted quieter things—a Sunday together with no urgency, a conversation that didn't dissolve into emojis, a shared silence that didn't feel strained.

Our conversations now were clipped, transactional at worst, hollowly affectionate at best. I had grown used to waiting for his calls, his attention, his affection—and in doing so, I had let my routines and joys wither. My flat, once my quiet haven, now felt like a waiting room. I cooked less, read less. Even the small things—my Saturday morning plant-watering ritual, my old jazz playlists, my half-finished sketchbook—all lay abandoned. I had built my days around him, and in doing so, erased myself.

Our needs were different, and somewhere we badly failed to acknowledge and respect them. We had started living *for* each other, but forgotten how to live *with* each other. In that compromise, our individualities had slowly frayed, and what remained was a version of love that felt more like obligation than choice.

I collected myself, took a deep breath, and let my heart go astray for a minute. We all need emotional addictions and more when thoughts of dying love have crept into our lives. You know when it's stale, and your love life has reached a point of impossibility.

****

Dhruv's presence was intoxicating—an entirely different energy from Atulya's steady, fatherly calm. Atulya commanded respect with quiet wisdom; Dhruv invited affection with effortless charm. Where Atulya had been a guiding hand, Dhruv was a spark—bright, unpredictable, and oddly magnetic. And strangely enough, he was warmest to me. Within just a day or two of joining, he'd added me on Skype and, without fail, would drop a message by evening: *Beer?*

We rarely talked office, he was particularly interested in sharing his love for theatre and the performing arts, and from there his stories of folk songs in Eastern Europe would start. I always played the patient, inquisitive listener. The depth and diversity in his stories were charming, and his skills as a raconteur were worth falling for.

His actions and his words rang in my mind as I gulped my waffle. His warm, avuncular smile made me feel safe, and the way he looked at me, with a patient gaze, made me feel loved. In just a few days, he had claimed a territory in my heart. As calls with Nikhil grew shorter, messages fewer, and our chats drifted into the terrain of formality, I began to feel the weight of the silence between us. And into that widening void, Dhruv slipped in—effortlessly, almost unknowingly—filling spaces I hadn't even realized were empty. In my dull life, he seemed to have come as a version of warm affection. And even after knowing that he could be my Medusa, and I turned into stone upon staring into his eyes, I wanted to stare into those eyes, and plunge into the deep shadows of guilt. If it was my destiny to become stone again, a part of me was eager to embrace that destiny. I wish I could erase that want off me.

He brought a whiff of newness into my life. No tricks this time, I didn't want to know his sexuality. And even if he were straight, I could live under the pretence of being loved. I could wrap my life in the smokes of his breath, and draw a hundred pictures of togetherness in the curves of his radiant smile.

Ah! And that was it, thoughts of an unjust love.

And Straight On from Morning

Dhruv was in his cabin when I reached the office. And little had I settled when my Skype window popped, notifying me of his message.

"My day started with an article of yours. I had no idea you wrote on life issues. Are there more things I am not aware of, and should know?"

I replied with an emoji, "But why were you looking for my article in the morning?"

"I was trying to find more about you, call it stalking, you may," a wink followed his message.

"Ahh, stalking, is that a part of corporate strategy too?" I asked

The very thought that he was trying to find out more about me excited me. It made me grin like an idiot.

"Well, it won't be wrong to call it stalking. I was looking at your Instagram profile, and came across these articles and your pictures too, which are equally great."

I sent a 😊.

"If I may ask, the guy in many of your past Instagram posts – is he your boyfriend?"

I was left befuddled. I wasn't expecting a personal question from him. I gaped at his cabin; he was still, eyes glued to the laptop.

"I think we talk better with a beer mug in hand," and a laughing emoji, "Skype conversations are so bereft of emotions."

"It's fine, I get that, you don't want to talk about your personal life. And we will have to miss our beer session today, as I need to see my cousins in the evening, but to make up for the beer session, we can do a lunch plan, in case you wish to." He typed.

"Lunch works fine; I need to go out for lunch anyway," I replied.

My subconscious stared at me blankly. I knew I was inviting trouble into my life. But there's always some worth in one-sided love; it comforts you when nothing else could. Seeing his answer, my mind brimmed with pleasure, and my face transformed with a ridiculous smile on it. Perhaps he might have noticed that as well. I was surely enjoying it, fixing myself to one face: living in a bubble to make myself oblivious to everything else happening in my life.

I needed a distraction, and he came as one, and if not him, I would have looked for someone else. My love life was failing, and all I wanted to do to rectify that was to create a parallel world where I could stay unperturbed.

The dried-up cocoon I had chosen to stay in had started making a cracking sound. I wanted to let myself free; unhitched from things that were before me, uncertain of the future, but able to rock my boat, spin my wheel, or dry the skin between my fingers. I was giving my soul a passage, an opening to let out, dance in the rains, get mesmerized by the golden hue of the fallen leaves, soak the chill in the air, and spread a lavish smile upon seeing young hearts meet and melt. It had to come out; it had stayed for long inside, protecting secrets, and was afraid of many consequences like an insecure child lost to war. It kept whining for itself and worrying for others. My heart bled, and my soul didn't feel it. My heart always waited for consensus. It's comforting, but sometimes the perception of consensus is also false. Now it tended to agree with different versions of the same verses. I wanted it out, so no questioning myself on little pleasures, and guilt trips.

It felt good…so carnal…so necessary.

"Does one o' clock sound good?" His message popped.

I grinned with excitement. I pursed my lips but was unable to hide my amusement.

"Sounds good! We can do Café Pluck, their continental offerings are good," I replied, "and they serve vegan food too, so it works for me," another smiley.

"I feel like zipping you up for your vegan jokes now." He wrote, followed by a teasing GIF.

"See, now is the right time to decide, you might end up in a vegan zone if you stay too much with me," I teased.

"I so wish I could use some of your tantrums for inspiration. And off the record, I won't mind being in the vegan zone if the food is tasty." I smiled at his reply, a genuine, genial smile.

***

I was used to feeling invisible, and mostly indifferent to it. I wasn't conventional, but I wasn't a rebel either. I had always kept my world carefully guarded, never letting too many people peer into the deeper recesses of who I was. I didn't open up easily—not because I was hiding, but because solitude felt familiar, almost sacred. I lived within a quiet halo of my own making, drawing strength from stillness, waiting for night to unfurl its spell—the moon casting its eerie glow, the hush settling like an old friend. And in that strange, enchanted silence, my thoughts would finally rise, unfiltered and alive.

This inner world shaped more than just my habits—it shaped how I loved, how I worked, how I let people in. With Nikhil, I had once believed I could merge that solitude with companionship. But slowly, I had blurred the line, pouring too much of myself into his chaos, trying to meet him in places where I didn't belong. I wasn't made for crowded evenings or endless conversations. I longed for depth over noise, for pauses over reactions. For years, I had kept myself hidden in the shadows of my being, where in a cozy setting lay Nikhil and I, and with us, all our random thoughts, wishes, and promises. It had been too long a night, as long as seven years, for us to live and rejoice in its subtlety. It's been too long.

I walked up to the pantry to make coffee, and looked out of the window. The sky, plastered with clouds, looked surreal. I could see it through the dried branches of *Amaltas,* cutting across each other like arms spread for blessings. I wondered how splendid the tree looks in summer, when it is in full bloom, and when everything around it is equally green. It still had a strange and lifting rhythm to it. It had started getting a little chilly, too, out of place for August. I wondered after some days, the sky would wear a blanket of smog in the notorious polluted winters of Delhi. And there would be no escape from that.

I looked out of the window intently at the trees, like I understood their movement. As if they confided their secrets in me. In days, the trees would have shed their leaves, and the breeze would come to a standstill. The chill would make life uncomfortable. But even in their ardent nakedness, the trees would evoke many thoughts, and catch me in a spell that would cause a lapse of time in a manner I'd never understood. An unheard poet in me would breathe, and probably live only in my Instagram posts, and life would be reduced to many such ephemeral stories.

This winter was to be long; Nikhil had hinted at a long schedule, a schedule that included a two-month stay in London. Thus, for two months, our relationship would be reduced to video calls. The present was nothing different, but there still was solace that we met once a month. I wish I had asked him to choose me over his career move, but I was never like that. I lived through when he chose to be in Africa for six months. I lived through the pain of separation because my heart consoled me that it was fine. Relationships should not be a drag on personal choices or aspirations. I sacrificed my wishes when he wanted to move to Mumbai, and now to London. I never stopped him, for I could never stop myself.

I took a deep breath. What I needed was time—and a generous dose of distraction—to return to work, to slip back into that practiced indifference that had become the emblem of my life. I looked around in want of one person I could trust, and cry out my heart to, but there was none around. My eyes met Dhruv's as he walked towards the pantry, always a delightful distraction.

"Don't tell me you drink this coffee; this will give me a reason to judge you," he jokingly said to me, pointing at the cup of machine-made coffee.

"Well, it's just that it is a quick way to coffee, unless someone agrees to whip some coffee and make me a nice cuppa," I replied in a sarcastic tone with an undertone of snobbishness.

He looked at me, an intense gaze accompanied by a comforting smile, almost prodding me to be at my seductive best.

"Put in some labour to get your caffeine. Take matters into your own hands. Machines are hopeless—they don't get the emotion that comes with a good cup of coffee."

He took out a hand grinder and a portable pour-over brewer from one of the shelves. I could see a maestro working his magic. The quality of any coffee goes to the roof when human attention is added to the equation, and at that moment, coffee enjoys its unwavering attention.

"Here you go, so see, sir, all you need is to take matters into your hands, and shape your coffee as you shape your thoughts," he said with a sense of pride, and offered me the coffee mug.

"Coffee, beer, EDM, what else interests you?" I asked, with an awkward smile on my face.

"Ahh! Now you are going down the dangerous road of getting to know me. It's a dangerous road where words and thoughts won't come to your rescue," he said, taking a sip.

I bent against the wall, in an easy position, looking to initiate another soulful conversation…

At exactly one o'clock, we started for Café Pluck. The road on which we started wheeling away took me far from the worries of the past to the promises of the future. He put on a Bryan Adams song; I smiled to hint at my concurrence. Soon, I saw the fading city in the mirror; we were wheeling past the crazy South Delhi to the airport road. It looked like it would drizzle, a wet August sky, I wished to chase the sun, or steal some sunlight and decorate it on his face, to see his face gleam again. He smiled, looking at me, silently asking me to share my thoughts. But right then, my thoughts were all his. His simplicity twinkled in my eyes, and his congeniality poured into my smile. As the car wheezed, and he lip-synced the songs, I tried gathering pieces of mine. Nothing matters when you are walking through time, all the colours seep out, and you float in a mirage of perpetual torment.

"You haven't spoken a word since we started from the office," he said.

I swallowed.

"You take me to be a chatterbox," and he gave me a puppy face.

"And you know I'm the worst person to be prodded for stories," I wish I could laugh louder than I laughed then.

He hid his unrest in another gracious smile.

"Tell me the last movie you watched, in a theatre," he asked abruptly.

"My bad, it has been quite a while since I have been to a theatre," I acknowledged. I am not much of a movie person.

"Seriously…then what do you do when your boyfriend comes to meet you?" He asked in a squeamish tone.

"Well, for a start, I cook something nice for him, we watch a show or movie, we make love, and we talk about our lives. Basically, I want to have an eyeful and heartful of him when he comes, so these plans of going out for a date, or a movie, seem like a nuisance."

"Do you not miss that carefree dating life?" He asked.

I had always been extremely protective of my personal life, but then, with him, I wanted to open up.

"Never thought so," I answered.

A brief silence followed, and then I asked him, "What about you, tell me about your life…are you single or with someone?"

"Oh! Don't ask about my dating life. My love life is jinxed; either things don't click, or it ends in a one-sided affair. My last relationship was some two years back, when I wasn't in India. I haven't been on a date after that," he answered with a flint of a smile on his face.

"Have you ever dated an Indian?" Yes, you have to be a lame duck to question that.

"Nope, my last was a Belgian. My higher education and early professional life are all from Europe. Well, is, 'Indians are more loyal' coming next to me?" He added quickly, blushing.

I nodded, grinning like a fool. He regarded me coolly, though his eyes were alight with humour.

"Do you believe in true love? I have increasingly started to believe that these days' love stories are lived as Instagram stories, up there for a day for your amusement, where it can betray reality, and then things slide as the reality of the relationship hits." He opined with a hint of pain and malice.

"Gosh! You are so obsessed with Instagram," the sulky schoolgirl in me spoke, hiding her distrust in a made-up smile.

He smiled brightly, getting the innuendo in the joke. And in an instant, the color rose in my cheeks as he batted an eyelid at me.

It was strange to begin with. He was so demonstrative in some ways, and so closed in others. He was right; he was protective of his personal life, unlike me, who was slowly learning to lay it bare.

We reached our place after a good ride of thirty minutes spent exploring ourselves, and some hidden layers of our lives. He gave the car keys to the valet and sauntered his way towards the hotel's lobby. There was an unmissable touch of command in his walk, a lovely slight wiggle in the hips, legs splayed, balanced shoulder swag, and small steps. It was kind of juvenile, with a tinge of bounciness and sexiness added to it. Looked like I was stalking in my way, and loving every moment with him.

Reaching the café, he asked, "So what do you want to order?"

"Take a breath, first you need to tell me if you like my find," I chuckled and rolled my eyes.

He blushed. From the corner of his eyes, I could see his comfort. Dhruv looked around impressively at the contemporary and stylish decor of the place.

"The place is nice, no doubt. This means I can easily trust your recommendations," he said quietly, his voice clipped.

"You want to try continental? I can suggest their croissants, the rest we can pick," I stopped and faced him, my eyes wide.

He pressed his lips into an uncompromising line, and said, "This is so chic, it almost looks like a date to me." he sounded jocund, but had the grace to look staid.

I could only manage to blush and look at him from the side. A wide smile spread on his face. That wasn't a date, but his question had taken me aback. I didn't want to get into that situation again, chasing a distant dream, like Icarus, for I felt too burdened with guilt to even flap wings.

After a minute-long debate in my mind on replying or not replying to his statement, I cheekily answered, "I don't even have an idea if I can or I would ask you for a date. I thought you wouldn't have seen nice places in Delhi, so I pulled up this plan,"

"Well, I can see the plan was quite well improvised upon," he smiled as he said, with his gaze set on me.

If that was a game, I wanted it to continue. It was my narrow escape from reality, an alternate universe where I could spread my wings without being burdened, and take my flight. I was still the Icarus, just that with Dhruv, I could think of soaring higher in the skies of my desire.

And I did try to give it a touch of a well-planned date. Not only did I choose the most comfortable corner to preserve our privacy, but also ordered the signature dishes from their gourmet retail good, starting with salads with oven roasted beets and citrus segments with balsamic dressing, followed by wood fried thin crust pizza, and ending with choosing from the wide array of teas they had. The service was quick, but I could have loved the wait too, watching him blush with pleasure, growing cheeky red in the cheeks to a blissful roll of his eyes as he cracked a joke.

There was a feeling of comfort set between us, as we drifted from conversation, life, philosophy, to world affairs. He could speak equally when he talked global environment as when he talked about life. And in the middle of a serious conversation, he could easily crack an easy joke, like a spirited schoolboy. It was so easy to put all your definitions of a perfect man on one side, and make this gregarious, spirited soul your love. It was so easy to find meaning in whatever was simmering between us, or whatever road we were gearing to take. It was so easy to find a soul in every random conversation we had, and equally easy to find a smile on his face.

I didn't try to gauge his interest in me; I wanted that warmth to stay and simmer, just like the poetic exuberance of September breeze—slow, soothing, and benevolent. The magic of misplaced feelings, the cuteness of love which doesn't long for a story, and dreams which know no beginnings—I was wrapping my life in the impossibility of a notion called one-sided love, and I was larky about it.

Dhruv called for the bill, so effortlessly chivalrous. Not in the fairytale prince kind of way, but in that quiet, genuine manner that makes you wish more people were like him.

"No, bill on the planner, or we split the bills," I objected.

"Hey, it's all good, lemme do it, and take it as my joining party, and I insist," Dhruv replied.

"You know I can insist too, and as far as the joining treat is concerned, you are ordained to pay for the vodka shots for everyone in the coming office party. And for today, we split, and I insist," I said persuasively.

He smiled his charming boy smile, and I felt like taking him in my embrace and drinking that smile, and decorating my soul with it.

We sauntered out of the café. It was almost four, almost a day taken off to know more of each other, a nice distraction from reality.

"I hope you don't need more detours," he said quizzingly.

"Oh, I am so sorry, I kept you out of your 'don't disturb me, I am formulating strategy' mode for such a long time," I teased.

As always, he smiled, just that time, he took me for a half hug and passionately rubbed my shoulders, as if putting a solemn flag on my being. My eyes met his, and I measured the depths of his eyes. I could almost imagine him holding my chin and locking himself in a kiss. My lips involuntarily opened to accommodate his, his eyes reached down to my parted lips, and with his hand, he fingered my hair. The world seemed to collapse before me, and all my being condensed in the little space between us. I had come unflinchingly close to him, so close that all boundaries evaporated in the smokes of our breaths. My being was tested, my inner goddess jived, and my flaneurial heart sang...that was my moment.

Dreams Mask Reality

I wanted to talk with Dhriti about the situation. She had been my soul keeper for seven years; best friend, guardian, and counsellor, always donning some hat to bring sanity and stability in my life. I wish I had told her then. It was Thursday, and Nikhil was to visit me over the weekend. I didn't want to have a talk when he was around; after all, our talk was to be about him, and our decaying love life.

Dhiriti and Aarya, now married, had been calling me for a long time to their apartment. It wasn't far from mine, just that I couldn't fix the meeting. I quaked at the thought of meeting them and talking about my life, and then with Dhruv around, I started to stay back longer in the office. For a loner like me, the office had always offered more solace than any other social setting. And then I was juggling between my work and my writing, and was finding it hard to steal time for myself. The office work was proving a bit too demanding to allow space for my writing, but then a little juggling, and time taken off any social interactions post office, proved a way to manage things.

Sensing my reluctance to take that extra effort to visit her, Dhiriti offered to come to my apartment. My apartment was just a manageable little place, perfect for my needs.

"Are these the new paintings you were talking about that day?" She asked, pointing at the two paintings set almost parallel to each other, with a lamp in the middle.

"That corner looked a little too empty to me, and I thought a slice of some chic African art would fit there. What do you think?" I asked, looking at her.

"You have an eye and the patience for these. Remember those days when you used to take me out for some shopping…ah! It has been so long, Anu. And this place looks so different from the last time, it seems like I came here ages ago," she said in her usual sarcastic tone.

I could guess she was upset. Aarya, Dhriti, and I had always been the closest people, back from our college days, and Nikhil was a year senior to us. So, in a way, we all were connected. Despite this long association, of late I had so ungraciously been avoiding meeting them.

"I wonder if it will be—can be—any more beautiful than this," murmured Dhriti, looking around her, with her loving, enraptured eyes of those to whom 'home' must always be the loveliest spot, incomparable to any other treasure or promises of the world.

"It wasn't long back, it's just that I keep changing the décor. I don't know if you ever noticed, I painted the walls twice in two years of my stay here, and then endless this and that, here and there; every corner is a story here," I replied, almost hugging her with adulation.

"I know you. And tell me how much are Nikhil's thoughts and inputs in this," she asked enthusiastically.

"To be candid with you, with this whole Mumbai thing, all these matters are off his head, and I have full control over what to do here. And trust me, that's for the better. But I do feel like single again," I said, smiling inwardly to myself.

Dhriti seemed to boldly examine me as I spoke, and after a minute-long silence, where she almost looked like gathering her thoughts, she said, "I get the issue in your life, but don't you think this is such a wholesome situation, no expectations, no relationship hassles, all the freedom to do what the fuck you want to do, and no worries? Sometimes relations restrict you, so don't let this constant feeling of singlehood crash you."

I chuckled, more at her excitement than the depths of the statement.

"Not really, but now that you have mentioned it, I believe I can look at this new grown singlehood differently," I smiled winningly.

It was said like a careless, unsophisticated statement; it meant nothing. But I knew there was value in her statement. Had I wanted, I could have told her about my dying, or let's just say dead relationship, and the fact that I was drawn to another guy. Deep down, I wanted to lay down the tempest shaping within me before her, but I chose to restrain myself from talking. I loved my demons, and nurtured them, and let them become potent and take control of my life. Darkness is intoxicating. It reveals one's deeper selves. Probably, I was finding everything too incomprehensible for even myself to talk about it with her. I was in a relationship that I knew had lasted its life, and it would be Panglossian of me to even consider that the relationship would survive, and at the same time, I wanted someone else, too, who often seemed within my reach. I was confused about how to react to the myriad of fizzling thoughts spinning in my head.

"Do you want to have a coffee?" I asked.

More than her, I needed a strong dose of caffeine to settle my unsettling heart.

"Who says no to such a generous offer?" She winked at me.

"And how is Nikhil? Is he coming soon?" She asked as I set the kettle on the gas.

"He is coming this weekend. He comes once a month, sometimes more. It's been terrible, and he is drowning in too much work. To be honest, I never wanted him to take this job, but you know he is so career-focused that sometimes I get the feeling that I am nowhere in his priorities," I basically complained.

She was leaning on the balcony balustrade, drinking in the enchantment of the sunset. The fine, purpling dye of sunset stained the skies, and the moon was rising. Remembrance wore a sweet and subtle spell over us. I got her coffee; she smiled at me, a restrained smile, as if some old memory had crashed in the tempestuous seas in her mind. Her eyes deepened into darkness. The spell of the dusk was broken for her.

"Is everything fine between you two?" She asked, half resentfully, half sorrowfully.

"Doesn't it seem to you?" I answered, with a rather overdone carelessness.

It felt like something alien had got into me, I wanted to speak, rather hug her and cry my heart out, but I didn't. I chose to swallow my insecurities, and with it the beasts shaping within me.

"You know if ever and whenever you wish to talk, I'm here to listen," decreed Dhriti, looking at me with utmost concern of a friend.

I knew that, and I smiled.

"How's your life? How well are you tolerating 'Mr. Never growing up', Aarya," I asked cheerfully.

"I believe I have seen all his shades now, there's nothing more exciting left. And for him, this guy has refused to grow up; he's still the teen lad of college days, who could leave everything to be with me. He jeers, flirts, throws tantrums, holds the same expectations; it seems I have literally been living my college life for the last seven years," she almost broke into a peal of loud laughter.

"That's Aarya for you, didn't I predict all of that?" candidly I had always been more worried about Aarya being able to survive the dangerously intellectual species that Dhriti was.

Deep down I knew Aarya, and his ability to shore up little pieces in life to create a halo of happiness around him. He would live in it, feed off it, nurse it, and bring his loved ones under the auspiciousness of that halo.

"I don't know if there are some nice things about it…but I really need a way out of this," added Dhriti, caressing her ring with that little smile, which always made me feel inexperienced and unknown to many things.

"You definitely know it more than me, don't you?" She smiled.

"I sometimes feel if I can ever live that life of carelessness. Sometimes it doesn't feel we are married. We aren't doing any couples' thing; it's like time never moved for us, and we are still fixated with that messiness of college romance, he is always eager to have dates, gifts, flowers, and surprises – you know sometimes it gets too much."

"I'd live your life any day," I said, looking deep into her eyes, "I wish I could get a piece of this in my life, the same old craziness, living for each other's smiles, those hours where you do nothing but cuddle each other. I feel that my entire life was just spent in fighting for my love, and now I question myself – what for," I added, feeling heavy.

"You both showed maturity when you had to," she came closer and put her hand on my shoulder.

"And our maturity killed the love," I looked into her eyes, the darkness set in her eyes met the depths of mine, "It always does."

"Nope the mature individuals did. You kept choosing little battles to win, with your family, with his family, with the world; when all you two could have done is chosen each other. Everything can wait, you need to give life some chance, not every person is ready to pick battles like you are, or probably you should choose someone who can stand by you as you take your indulgence to activism mode. Nikhil wasn't ready for that, and you always pushed him." She said in a grave tone.

"You think it was because of that?"

"I don't know, no one knows. I don't think even you and Nikhil have that answer. It's what I feel; you people live in different dimensions, and are not willing to step down from your claimed positions, to let things work. There is too much desperation and dependence, and when he got a chance to break some bonds and live a life for himself, he chose to do that. Aren't you doing the same by getting absorbed in your work and writing?" She added rather sulkily, and suddenly I heard my inner voice ringing out clearly.

I nodded in acknowledgement. It was never easy for Nikhil and I. We needed our space—we needed to find solitude in our shells. Did it get too difficult at times to carry the baggage of our thoughts? Didn't those elements, however trivial they may seem, define us? Or was that too difficult, or rather unnecessary to remain an individual when we were together? Did the 'we' in our relationship overpower the 'I' to satisfy the 'you'?

We are complex creatures, beaten by the tidal waves of our emotions. Some like Nikhil choose to live at the edges, and some like me choose to face it, get beaten by the veracity and vivacity of life; we reorganize ourselves after every fall, and take another step, only to be beaten again. Nikhil wasn't I, I wasn't Nikhil, and we never tried hard to understand who the other person exactly was or wanted. Our 'I' destroyed the 'us'.

"Are you getting what I am trying to imply?" Dhriti's words dragged me out of the silence of my thoughts.

I looked at her and gave a solemn smile. I was getting what she was trying to imply, I had got that all along.

She came close to me, and wearing a sagacious smile, murmured, "You can't fight for your love when you are fighting other battles."

And there is no greatness in fighting battles lonely. Five years back, I fought a battle at my home when I came out of my shell. It took months for the people I loved the most to come to terms with my identity. But I chose candor over coy. I wanted Nikhil to do the same in his family, but he couldn't. My past is decorated with my struggles, wrestling with my inner demons, queering the pitch for the entire community, and consistently trying to make things last in my love life. It had been a heck of a struggle, and I had started feeling tired of making efforts to make things right.

I looked at her with concern in my eyes, as she tried to find answers in me, which probably never existed.

On the other side of the road, a few tree trunks shone as candles, as the moonlight pierced their way through the thresholds of those old, giant trees. The play of light and shadow seemed to speak of mysteries, too profound to be felt. Beneath the mysterious green, past and future melted in death and mystery, masked by serenity, constantly absorbed, but never passed on. There are worlds within worlds, churning, existing parallels, bringing abundance and catastrophe upon the unalarmed mortal beings. I wanted to laugh before I shrank back to gloom, waiting for the night, to be in unnatural solidarity with the mystery that drapes these greens, and to embrace my unknowns.

***

Nikhil and I were living through a long-distance relationship. It had been two years since we had been meeting every month. Sometimes it became once in two months. Our chats were getting shorter, calls rarer, and video chats once in a long while. The distance between us was palpable and gaping. The course of life hadn't been easy for those two years. I felt a huge void. Blame it on distance, work stress, not having enough conversations, my constant mood swings, or the polar opposite personalities we had. The truth is, blaming would not have changed the fact that the seemingly perfect relationship was showing signs of its imperfection. And we failed to realize that, and inch by inch, our imperfections devoured us.

I dragged our relationship until it became too heavy for me to handle alone, and I started feeling vulnerable and drawn to feelings I needed the most. I felt lost, lost in the search to find something to rediscover my soul. I wondered if I could ever stop searching.

I was tired and beaten and needed a hug to hold me from splintering into hundreds of pieces. All I needed was for someone to embrace me tightly, come close, and whisper in my ears, 'all will be good'. And Nikhil wasn't there for me to say that.

Deciding to let go of the relationship and losing Nikhil gave me a feeling of freedom. The pain accompanied by this loss seemed addictive, and evocative; and I was drawn to the feeling like the sunflower is to the sun, or water is to the crevices in the ground. I did everything to enwrap myself in its nothingness.

I often tried reflecting on my love life and wondered what went wrong, or what could have happened differently. Ours was a seemingly perfect story caught in its imperfections. It wasn't one event or a series of events; it was just something, somewhere, somehow, that happened, and kept happening. I had no clue of it, or was aware of it. And with time, things got rough and unamenable.

Whenever Nikhil came to Delhi, something between us would quietly realign. Conversations flowed more easily, the silences felt less strained, and for a little while, it felt like we were still us. His presence had a way of smoothing over the rough edges, of stitching shut the questions I had long buried. With him around, things simply worked—at least on the surface. I could believe, for a moment, that we were fine.

But the moment he left, the distance returned—heavier, more pronounced. The unanswered questions came rushing back, louder than before. Was I the only one still holding on? Did he notice the cracks, or had he already moved past them? I was left sifting through our time together, unsure of what was real comfort and what was carefully constructed illusion. And in that hollow quiet, I couldn't escape the feeling that I cared more, felt more, wanted more—while he remained a beautiful echo, always just out of reach.

When he was gone, I unraveled. My mind turned into a storm—waves of longing crashing against shores of resentment. I felt needful. I wanted to hold onto something solid, something real, but all I had were fragments of what we once were. And the truth—the one I barely admitted to myself—was that it wasn't just about him. It was about the growing emptiness that followed me everywhere, even into the brightest rooms.

"What are you doing here alone? And you look so pale? Is there something troubling you?" Dhruv's words came as a calm, gentle interrogation, despite the suffocating fear that was engulfing me.

My brow furrowed as if completely taken aback by his presence.

"I was going to make coffee for myself, would be happy to brew some for you," I looked at him and smiled. I took a deep lungful of air, in an attempt to calm my panicked breathing, and with another smile, expressed my yes to the proposal.

Dhruv moved towards the burner and took out the utensils from the shelf. He reached out to the kettle and, with a shaking hand, filled it from the faucet. As I saw him put some soya milk to boil, my breathing eased. He remembered; he'd ordered a supply of soya milk for vegans in the office. These moments, when you wish you had the switch to stop everything around, and cling to your boy, like in a timeless wrap, with everything melting between two smiles, and you can gaze deep into those eyes and discover the honesty of the soul. Everything was so out of control, like some old map where you need stars to guide your way. I smiled as I heard the milk hiss in the kettle.

"You think a lot," Dhruv said with absent, bemused curiosity.

"I have lots of time at my disposal to think, and isn't that what I am paid for?" He didn't look content with my reply.

"I have noticed you many times. This narrowing of brows is not because of work, it's something else you keep within you," he said as he inclined his head the other way, giving me a piercing look.

I looked at him with anxiety building inside me, my inner demons waiting to be set free with every word. Even if I wanted, I couldn't have opened the bare irony of my life. A seven-year-long relationship haunted by a tumultuous past, and defeated by its desire to live and grow.

"If it is about something in life, I will suggest not letting emotions and fears guide you, and being rational about your future. If you wish to take an off and unwind, you should do that. And all I want is for you to figure out the best way to be able to look beyond everything that's troubling you. Can I ask you for this?" Of course, he could.

He held me with his steady gaze. That was perhaps the most chilling and sobering sight I had seen in the course of a few months, after my life had started exploding with a series of unwanted and uncontrollable events. The vague fuzziness I was suffering from evaporated. His words had done what they always did: dragged me out of my unsteady state, to a state of normalcy, a steady feeling, a feeling of belonging, a feeling that someone was there to hold when I felt myself break into a thousand words.

"Hey, my boy, give me a hug now," and I wrapped myself in his warm embrace, my heart squeezed and twisted.

This was possibly all I wanted at that time, a gentle hug that could wash me of my fears.

"Just don't worry, and don't feel bad, we all go through a lot. What's important is to know how to come out of these situations," he consoled.

Compassion, love, and despair all swelled in my heart. I felt a sense of desperation to have him in my life. Those two chapters of life, happening simultaneously, one pushing me away from my past, and the other pushing me towards an uncertain future, pushed me to the brink of a state of confusion.

We unwrapped, and he offered me a cup of coffee. He knew how to lift my mood.

He blinked once.

"What would you like me to say?" He said softly, as if to gauge the depths of my frittered soul.

"Nothing, all you said was quite heartening. I just hope I can put those words to action," I answered, and he nodded.

I looked at him, enthralled. He fixed his gaze on me, and a small, assuring smile set on his gleaming face. He kept his gaze fixed on me, smiling between the sips of coffee he took. He kept his cup down, and moved a step towards me. My heart was in my mouth.

"You look so good when you smile. You should keep smiling, I love to see you like that," he whispered.

Oh! I didn't want that, his words had the potency to push me down the rabbit hole – oh, I did want that – madly. I was in a state of utter confusion, and he tended to leave me in a more confused state with every conversation. I tore my gaze away from his spellbinding look.

The swelling tide of emotions, died.

Dhruv headed over to his mobile, and moments later the heavenly sweet, soulful voice of Sinead O'Conor filled the small room. He loved the intensity of her songs, and sang along as she sang *Nothing, but you.* I flushed, gaping at him. What was he trying to suggest? Was that an attempt to bring peace, or put some spell on me? His look had changed, the levity disappeared, and it appeared dark and intense now, holding seas of desire. His proximity was overwhelming for me, making me so vulnerable. There was a familiar pull in that stare, and my nerves goaded me towards him. I had to hold myself. I managed to stay sane and didn't make a move. His heat was warming my skin, and I chose to resist that.

That Still Small Voice

The next day at office, I tried to distance myself from Dhruv. He was getting onto my nerves like an old memory that keeps coming back to haunt you. I watched him from my seat, he was engrossed in some tiring work, I could tell from his wide and intense eyes. That was ridiculous, I was swooning over him like a preteen girl. Something in him was making me forget the connection between my brain and heart. I wanted to just plug in my earphones, listen to music and not look at him, but it was more my peering nature than concern that made me decide against my will to go and see him. Gosh!

"Hope I am allowed to disturb you," I murmured in a low tone.

He smiled, his eyes lit with delight at seeing me. "I wish you could disturb me."

"You look vexed—something happened?"

"Not much, I was looking at these old balance sheets, we seem to be going down the rabbit hole. We need a complete rejig of our business strategy, and I am still trying to measure the amount of cooperation I can expect from everyone, considering I have just joined two weeks ago. But some things need to change, right?" He looked at me for assurance; I smiled, not so surprised. He took a step towards me and, leaning against his desk, he asked, "What would you do in my situation?"

"Talk it through and lay out my plans before them. Don't expect people to get the details, but make it clear that it's for them. No one hates a good business."

"Frankly, I don't want this place to become an out-and-out chasing-for-commercial-gains place. This place has a voice that shouldn't die." He smirked, amused and incredulous, and continued, "I want more engagement in all our shows, just the way you have on yours. We shouldn't be chasing stories; we should be living them. We have been creative so far, but not creatively engaging. And I can see a lot of resistance in implementing what I wish to; this place has lived in a good way, but not so viable." I couldn't make out if that was an outright insult to the business strategy we have had, or a logical explanation for our uninspiring balance sheets.

"You are right; this place has lived in a way. People feel creatively charged here, but commercial interests cannot be ignored. May I suggest that you go around and get to know people here more, and let them know you? Go sit with them and get acquainted. It won't be hard. And when they see the soft you, it won't take them much time to adore and trust you," I said calmly. He listened intently to every word.

We talked about his concerns and plans for another half an hour, and then he suggested something that opened the floodgates of my emotions. "It is believed that the verdict on decriminalisation of Article 377 will come next week. I want you to run your show for longer hours that day. Take the commands, our channel should stand as a voice of the vulnerable. No debates, no opinionated shows, let people break their story. You capture the rapture, emotions, ideas, and talk about what comes after the verdict. Be free to hold the mirror to society. And feel free to put everything the way you want. I don't want creativity in this, I want this show to be about empathy and spontaneity, and about everything our channel stands for," he declared with passion.

My eyes illuminated with enthusiasm, deep down, I wanted to do that. For a long time, I had taken this stride of liberty and justice forward on my show, and at that juncture, when everything was looking to change, I wanted to be there, right in the centre, with my arms open to embrace the stories. The notion intrigued me and I felt like making it more than a velleity.

"Do you like the idea?" He solemnly asked.

"I love it. It's soulful. Thanks for your support." I could feel that air of freedom in me as I said this. That would be historic for India, a move towards acceptance and appreciation of diverse thoughts, and paving the way for a society where people were not criminalised for their choices, love was appreciated, and diverse ideas were welcome. I could see a day where mornings are not close reminders of who we are, no need to hide the real us, and not unclothe ourselves from the nightwear in which we were we and get into our day corporate attire, in which we are as others perceive and define us, hiding our real identity in the sleek, polished, straight look.

My mind sauntered through the memories from different phases of my life, from childhood, college, job, and the feeling of isolation, emptiness, and weariness associated with all these phases.

"Would you like to share your story of coming out to your folks?" He asked. For a minute, I was taken aback. I had no answer to that; putting your struggles out to the public wasn't easy, and I wasn't sure if I was prepared.

He guessed my reluctance. "As I said, spontaneity will be the sauce of our show, so be there and do what you like. And if at any moment you feel that you can share your story, then you probably can. I hope people can relate better, but you be the judge of that. What I can say with utmost certainty is that your show will instill courage in many to appreciate their identity and be proud of it."

I nodded, reluctance visible on my face. He came close to me, leaned close, and whispered, "It will be a long and hopeful day, and we will go out for drinks after that."

"Long, hopeful and tiring," I corrected him, and subtly quashed his drinks plan. "Well, for now, I am happy that you appreciate it." I looked at him and gave a shy smile.

"We'll see. But before the weariness kicks in, stash in as much happiness and hope as you can. This is just the beginning," he said with calmness in his eyes. He was right, it was just the beginning, a step taken. Many battles were yet to be fought to attain equality.

The entire next week was going to be busy and full of action and dialogue across the social, intellectual, and political circles. But the entire issue needed to move from these circles to our drawing rooms, common people moving beyond changing their DPs on social media to show solidarity with queer individuals, parents understanding when their kids decide to come out, friends being supportive and open when one among them decides to open up, movies made with queer characters as protagonists and people watching them with open minds, a neutral, supportive discussion in companies' drawing rooms on diversity and inclusivity, and straight friends and colleagues not feeling uncomfortable when a queer friend wishes to hug them—the road to inclusivity was long and weather-beaten.

The dialogue needed to come out of those wraps it had long been kept in and go beyond the set gender binaries. And the dialogue had to go far beyond decriminalisation, to encompass marriage equality, joint bank accounts, adoptions, recognition as a partner in will, and surrogacy, to transsexual rights.

There are numerous stories hidden and suppressed in our larger desire to fit things within the gender binaries—we remain invisible to these expressions, these ideas, and these lives. And we fail to understand that we can't define these contours, and till the time we choose to do that, we will have these stories of mute cries and silent longings.

Dhruv felt we could do something about that, and the beauty of the notion had always intrigued me. And not because I had lived those notions, but also because it was too diverse and beautiful to let remain uncaptured. I was in from the moment Dhruv shared his idea. I only needed a format, and his mind to work on it with me to give shape to that program.

But before that, there was a weekend to live. Nikhil was coming back to town, and I had never faced a more difficult phase in our love life than that one. Our relationship was dying, or probably dead, and I had the task of burying it.

Venus in an Embrace

I decided to bask in the amber sunset radiance under a pale sky set in an inviting mix of rose and blue. The distant monuments by the Hauz Khas Lake were burnished bronze and their long shadows barred the green waters of the lake. Around them, a little wind sang, and in it there was a note of impending rain. I needed to clear my head of many thoughts that had abducted my sanity. And yet I sat there, flummoxed, as if some ominous prophecy had been fulfilled.

No, there isn't a bigger loss than going through this state of uncertainty, where a part wants you to hold onto the vestigial of your relationship, and the other part wants to start afresh. I dragged myself along the stretch by the lake. That entire month had been difficult; it had never been that hard before. I wanted to cave in to my deep conscious, having got tired of trying to make things work with Nikhil.

I looked at the clouds. They looked like an apparition in the dark, intense sky. The night slowly inched its way, hiding deep mysteries under its embrace. I took a lungful of air; the dullness in the air kind of made me sick. I sauntered back to the hip streets of Hauz Khas village. I badly needed a drink, or loud music, or both. I wanted to dissolve in the dissonance of my emotions.

I stopped, took my phone out, and scrolled through the Instagram account of Dhruv, smiling as I looked at every frame as if, through his pictures, I was invited to be privy to his deeply personal moments. That moment, I felt boundaries dissolve, like everything started and stopped existing simultaneously; like in that moment, time took off and reality and fiction came together to make sweet love. With a certain ease, I stepped out of one life and into another, from one uncertainty to another. I smiled, a deeply satisfying smile, like a lonely stoner who had found a way to merge in the loneliness of the night. I walked towards a café to have a drink and pacify my tempestuous mind.

I was yearning for the long night to pass and the morning to come with some notes of hope. I didn't know if I needed some hope or clarity or a solemn assurance. I shook my head. I felt world-weary, but I was enjoying the serenity of the night. A walk through the boisterous alleys of Hauz Khas, and then a little distance more to my home. It was a longer walk that night. I cared not to switch on the lights when I reached home. Art pieces cast elongated shadows across the stark white walls of the plain room. Moonlight shone through the windowpanes.

I collapsed on the couch with my head straight and raked a hand through my hair; a tell-tale sign that I was worried. I scrolled through the messages shared between Nikhil and me over that fortnight, the agitated replies, a certain sign that things had moved beyond a stage where they could be repaired. I waited for closure with a longing heart. I had turned flaccid, and the bags below my eyes sagged. Stress had corroded me. The last seven nights had been long and lonely, and no one to console me except for some occasional messages from Dhriti and calls from Aarya. Communication with Dhruv was still formal, and with my life on an uncertain hangar, I couldn't convince my mind to take a chance, even though my heart coveted that.

I lived such a contrast in life. I had to be calm, composed, and unaffected when I was with people, while in reality, I wanted to run around, screaming and crying. Storms brewed in those dark eyes of mine. And there was no escaping it; every night, those words *'I don't think it is working'* resonated in my head. I wanted to run away, and yet I held on, the last attempt, as they say, or closure as I saw it. I needed answers. I had lived every bit of my relationship with Nikhil like a dream, and there's nothing more depressing than the death of a dream.

I made myself tea, flipped through pages of an unread novel, surfed through Netflix—nothing worked. It was nine in the night, and I looked nothing close to being able to spend that night. And in utter desperation, I called Dhruv.

"Hey, sorry, I was just feeling low...and I thought we could talk." Words struggled to come out of me. My eyes were wet, my mouth dry.

"Hey, you do sound upset. You were upset this evening, too. Tell me what the issue is," he said with a note of concern in his voice. Then he spoke again, "Wait, actually, just hold on; message me your address, I'll come down. We live close by. Just don't worry."

I waited eagerly for him. To pacify my mind, I sat down on a low overstuffed couch, picked up a six-string guitar, and started to play. I was never adept at playing guitar; I merely toyed with the instrument, running a slide up and down and picking out a series of notes almost like scales. I found it relaxing and therapeutic. The guitar almost seemed to cry, and I hit the right notes; slowly, the toying became more serious and took real form.

I was soon playing a melody that seemed to haunt me with its need to be played. A few scales more, the tone almost set, when the doorbell rang. He was early, I thought.

"How are you doing?" He asked with a hand pressed to my cheek. I wasn't expecting this note of physical intimacy from him. In actuality, I loved it; it had been days since someone's touch had felt so immersive. I nodded my head.

"Nothing. I was just feeling lonely," I said, a soft smile spread over my face.

"It's okay, I'm here now. You can talk to me if you wish to." He ran his fingers through my short hair and brushed it ineffectually. I felt a little uneasy. He could guess that. "Wait, let me make you some coffee, that's the least I can do to ease you." He smiled his usual relaxed smile.

I got back to the couch and started toying with the guitar, as he busied himself making us coffee. As I tried setting my notes right, my nostrils could catch the scent of a rich and delicious-smelling coffee wafting across the room. The scent tingled my taste buds.

"I can smell something great in the making," I called tentatively, then smiled when he spun around towards the sound of my voice. I could feel a change in me, from my darker me to the one eager to embrace some life.

He broke into a boyish grin and replied, "I have made a full pot here, so no stopping you from indulging in more than one cup of coffee. And let this aroma bring you out of that 'lonely me' mode."

"Your company has done half the trick." I chuckled to myself, the little blush on my cheeks not fading away as he glanced over his shoulders.

"Love it. Hope coffee does the other half." He offered me my mug of coffee and sat next to me on the couch. "Now, tell me what's troubling you?" He asked, staring into the mug cradled in my hands.

"You know things are on the verge of breaking between Nikhil and me. That's making me feel... I have no idea what I want," I answered slowly.

"That's an interesting way to put it," he mused. "I can get it, these personal issues affect us gravely, graver than what a simple coffee can cure." His dark eyes twinkled as he joked. I felt a little heat rise in my cheeks with his words.

"You know, Anuj, I seriously don't know what to say here, I feel like a biased judge here." He came closer and muttered in a deeply affectionate tone, "See, I don't want things to remain this topsy-turvy for you. An easy answer to this is you need to get closure and probably move on with someone who can understand you and remain close to you," he added, clasping my hand, wearing a compassionate smile.

"I don't know exactly. I feel so confined here, and not sure for how long now. I just want to get out of here. But somehow, everything around me—and inside me—feels stuck in this same dull shade of gloom. Like I've been living in grey for far too long. I am not sure if I will ever try to get into another love story."

Dhruv reached across and patted one of my knees. "For a person as sweet as you, love will walk into your life, right from that door," he said, pointing at the door, and a reassuring smile spread across his face. I smiled too, though my mind was still focused on the hand which had come close to caressing my knee instead of a casual pat of reassurance.

I took the last swallow of my coffee and placed the cup on the floor. I looked at him intently, his smiling, assuring face. I inched closer, clasped his hand, and put my head on his shoulder. He put his hand across my shoulders and cuddled me in a warm, poetic embrace. "I am there for you," he whispered in my ear.

I could feel a connection then, something too profound to be defined, something deeper than most definitions and warmer than many feelings. I wanted to scream my feelings out loud, but I held the words to myself. I wanted to feel the agony of those unsaid words, or probably bask in the warmth of the combined effect of his embrace and the deep wells of his intense eyes. Endless tunes ran through my head as we remained in our embrace. The mysterious night threw open the gates of memories, and I recapitulated every moment spent with Dhruv. I reviewed my encounters with him to figure out just where and when my feelings changed from idle curiosity to…what was it then? Infatuation? Or probably a deep crush that cocooned a desire to turn real.

"Either start afresh, or close this existing chapter with your boyfriend; don't drag this. And you know I am there for you." He clinched me tightly and snugly as he spoke. We remained locked in that embrace for some time, when he broke the silence and whispered, "I love you." In my reaction, I inched closer to him, loosening all my guilt in that reaction; no words were said, no glances shared, but in that tiniest of moments, our hearts melted.

***

"I am so glad I could muster the strength to say this," he said. "I thought I would just keep it locked inside me."

I listened intently. We were on the balcony, overlooking the deserted streets. Another round of coffee. He held my hand. Each time he held my hand, images flooded my mind of his hands holding me much more intimately, and I wondered if, somehow, he sensed my imaginings. I smiled, breathing in the ecstasy of the moment.

"The view is spectacular from here," he breathed.

"That was one of the primary reasons I got this house," I replied, a smile spreading on my face. I looked into his eyes, and they held their charm. At that moment, I desired to melt into his arms. He chuckled and brushed his hands against mine. I turned back to the railing to drink in more of the view. He moved close behind me; I could feel his warm breath on the nape of my neck. I felt a sudden, tingling sensation down my spine. But I stayed unmoved.

He tangled his hands in my hair and softly played with them. "I always loved your hair," he said in a low, husky voice. I laughed a little nervously. With one arm around my shoulders, he led me back across the room and murmured, "I am famished. Should we order something?"

"Or I can quickly make something for you?"

"Your something means salad," he laughed.

"You are with a vegan," I exclaimed, with a note of badinage in my voice.

"A hot vegan, writer, and activist, I should start believing in God and his miracles again," came the reply.

"I had no idea you were an atheist."

"Call me agnostic."

As we talked, I made a light salad of romaine lettuce, almond slivers, and raisins in a wine vinegar dressing to start with. To go along with this, I prepared some quinoa porridge with beans, nuts, and broccoli. It didn't take me much time to prepare these super nutritious bowls for him.

As we ate, he put me at ease with his uncontrived interest in who I was and what I was about. We explored dimensions of our lives we had never talked about, and yet it seemed there was so much more to know about each other.

"You know, I won't come into your life if things get settled with your boyfriend. I know, no one can ever forget their first love. I respect that," he said as he poured some beer into my glass.

"Thanks. Though a part of me always wanted to break free, even much before you came into my life. That part has just got a little more convincing now." I chuckled almost to myself.

"You know, I'm an old-school romantic, and I believe in those fairy-tale, true love stories. For me, this connection is the purest thing possible." He winked at me, took me in his arms, and planted a feather-soft kiss on my forehead.

"I used to think that, but then realised that sometimes even fairy-tale stories fall apart, or probably they were never fairy tales to start with, just some grand, soothing, magical illusions." I held my thoughts for a moment, and then, directing my eyes back to him, I asked, "May I ask what happened to your love story? How did that fall apart?"

"Well, it never did, I was with him till he breathed his last," and the texture of his voice changed. "He used to talk like you, of bringing a change in the world, those piecemeal steps. He was my first love, and so far the only one. I never felt like that for anyone until I saw you. You are similar to him in so many ways; talking with you is like living those moments again—the similar chirpiness, the gay abandon, the spirit of freedom, always carrying novelty, strong ideas, and convictions. That always enthused me. After his death, some three years back, I bid goodbye to his family and moved back to India, spent a year in Mumbai, and now Delhi. I have not dated or even thought of dating since his death." He turned gloomy as he recounted his memories.

"Hey, cheer up, this crying department is mine!" I laughed and played with his all-so-messed-up hair. He laughed with me, took my hands in his, and caressed them softly from the inside of my wrist to my fingertips. I trembled a little as the sensations of his touch travelled with electric speed to my core. He truly was an old-school romantic, and I kind of loved that.

"It's been a long time, but I still feel burdened by that loss. I still see myself going to his grave, saying prayers in his name and comforting his family," he replied with a heaviness in his tone. His eyes were wet. I had never before seen such a soft side to him. Possibly, I was coming face to face with the meaning of loss in life, and in that moment, mine seemed so tiny in front of his. Call it an innocuous gesture, or my overactive hormones; I gave him an affectionate squeeze.

It's such an uneasy feeling, finding these fragments of life in each other. You read, you listen, you learn, you appreciate, but at moments, this knowledge means nothing compared to what you feel. These emotions are such fragile and contagious things, make us weep and laugh for strangers, and with loved ones, bring you closer to them, so close that you start getting a whiff that you were always inseparable.

At that moment, I felt heavy inside because of the death of a person I had never known. And next to it, another feeling rose, a feeling of hope, when he talked of being open to his partner's family. Nikhil wasn't open to his family, and I didn't exist for his family or close friends. For the world, we were just two friends from college who were hanging out together. You may not agree, but the feeling that you are nobody's nobody kills you from the inside.

I looked at him, this morose side of his. Feeling a bit reckless myself—an uncanny combination of loss of a relationship and euphoria of having a man I wanted to love ever since he came into my life, into my arms. It had also been a long time since both of us had been in a relationship—he a loner, and I lived in the shadow of a relationship. In the dim light of the room, Dhruv looked every inch a sex god, and resisting temptation seemed downright stupid.

I inched closer so that I could feel his warm breath against my face. He resisted, drew a little further, and said, "Don't you think we should wait for tomorrow, lest something happens and you change your mind, and—"

"And do you want to say, we shouldn't do something we'll regret tomorrow?" I tweaked his nose. He was a gentleman in every possible way. "And what if I tell you that my relationship, or whatever is left of it now, was over the moment I realised I could have you? Our kiss will validate that I took the right decision."

His lips were inviting, warm, and lush against mine, and then there was my pliant body pressed against his. Involuntarily, his arms moved and pulled me closer. My thirst deepened as his mouth sank deeper into mine. A million desires that he left throbbing, a million words left unspoken—read, unread—all melded into my flesh. And the more intensely we kissed, the more it left me feeling wanted, ablaze in his thoughts, all flowing through my eyes, weaving stories of timeless love, hope, and promise. As if I were looking for my dark hero to grant me absolution, wrap me in his inviting embrace and embalm all my pains.

He rubbed his thumb at the nape of my neck. He was itching to make love with me, but he suppressed his urge. Taking a deep breath, I reached for another kiss. His eyes didn't leave mine and he swallowed and his lips parted.

"You are my Venus," he murmured.

I clasped his face in my hands, tipped his head up and kissed him. He groaned low with pleasure. I was intense, and before I could realise, he had taken over control. His body was cradled against mine, his hand exploring my body while his lips rained down pleasure on my thirsty soul. His hand trailed from my thigh, along my belly, to my chest, squeezing, kneading and pulling me enticingly. I had been thirsty for this intensity for almost a year.

Our lips parted, and he softly murmured, "I want to be with you and live a life together. And this time around, I want a fairy-tale romantic story that doesn't meet an end." I smiled my concurrence. I ran my fingers across his face; his gaze was penetrating and I could feel the intensity of his emotions as I touched his so ravishing lips. I reached for the hem of my shirt and lifted it over my head, and then I did the same with his shirt. He gazed at me, bemused and breathless, and my eyes explored his bare body, trying to penetrate into his bare soul.

And he took me again. I closed my eyes and moaned, relishing his answering moan as he kissed me. I was getting lost in him—it was intoxicating to the exclusion of everything else around me. All my worries were obliterated. Nothing else seemed to matter. My blood sang in my veins, throbbing loudly, almost in perfect synchronisation to our panting breaths. I buried my hands in his hair, consuming him at the same time, enjoying the taste of his erupting feelings.

I so wanted that, to let go off all my insecurities and worries and lie in his possession. He grinned down at me, his lips parted, eyes dark and full of promise. He squeezed me in his arms and, leaning over me, rubbed his nose against mine. I felt luxurious in his arms. His eyes fixed on my face, fluctuated up and down between the void of my eyes and the wetness of my lips, covering the distance in the most obvious manner of desires and dreams.

With Nikhil, I started feeling that the distance between our breaths had been some light years, that time looked chained and unable to move, and that love, ephemeral, short-lived, or whatever tiny shred of it, had become illusory.

"I never knew it will turn out so leisurely beautiful. I was afraid to ask you," he murmured, and kissed me softly, gently biting my lower lip.

"I am sure you knew it can. I who harbored feelings for you. And I guess I was pretty obvious," I answered, and he smiled a luxuriant smile.

"Right now I want to just lie down, spooned to you. Let that be my life," he breathed, a solemn smile stretching on his face as some benediction.

I smiled at his ingenuity and made a funny little grimace. It was difficult to comprehend the gravity of his statement. "Let this grow. Let's not be in a rush to give it a name. It will find a name and space for itself." I leaned across and kissed his bare shoulders. "Probably I can get you some wine, and then we can pour ourselves in some more feelings."

"I'd prefer a beer instead, if there is some in the refrigerator."

I answered him with a twinkle in my eyes and grabbed two pints of beer from the refrigerator.

***

My head rested on his chest, his arms wrapped around me. My fingers were buried in his unruly hair, and we lay like that the entire night. The sunlight entered the room through the windows and woke me, but I wanted to remain cocooned in his arms and enjoy the quiet afterglow of making love with him. It was a quiet hangover, of both beer and love, and there was a shade of sweetness in the fine epiphany I had had the previous night. The sweet guy in me was attached to this world by a few slender threads that could break painlessly. They took their time to break, but they broke, as painlessly as imagined.

I got up, lazily and unwillingly. I felt a soothing, satisfying serenity. It was like coming to know oneself after a long time. Dhruv kissed my hair and rested his head on my shoulders. "I love you," he murmured.

I smiled, basking in the afterglow, and dug my fingers in his hair. "I love you too," I said softly.

"When is your ex coming today?" He asked, as I sat back down on the bed.

"Oh! So he is my ex now," I exclaimed teasingly.

Dhruv came closer and squeezed me into a loving hug. "If not, then make sure you make him one, and start this new life with me. After last night, I wish to lose all my goodness and turn selfish," he said, taking my hands into his. I pursed my lips but was unable to hide my amusement. It seemed so strange that a man who I knew no more than some conversations in the office and glances across from our seats, held so much pull on me. And I enjoyed that pull and wanted it to stay.

"We are meeting in the evening for coffee. He will be staying with his cousins. And to answer your question, we are formally over. This would be our last meeting," I replied, the last part of the sentence with an intense certainty. I reached for my phone and showed him the chat I had had with Nikhil. "You may read it…I believe you deserve that."

"I don't know what to say, I somehow feel sorry for you, though I don't know if I should."

"Hey idiot, don't be. It was destined. The bridges between us had been burnt long back; we were just hopelessly carrying the charade. Perhaps this is the time to relieve ourselves of that burden too." I grinned. I came closer and pursed my lips against his. He had come a long way, as had I, in such a short period. With all the fucked-up stuff of my past life, at times I kept losing sight of the simple, honest journey I wanted with him. A solemn kiss was needed to pull me back from my dark, haunted life to the pleasant present.

"I will let you sort this out for yourself, but know I am always there for you." I smiled and nodded my head at his sincerity.

"And as appealing as that idea is, I want us to do a dinner together, perhaps tomorrow if you get too tied up in sorting things out today, and start our life with just one promise—that we will never let love go less in our lives." His mouth pressed in one line as he declared his love in perhaps the holiest of ways I could have imagined.

I looked at him, my eyes wet, his full of promise. I wanted to roll my eyes, take him in my arms, and use some ancient magic to freeze time. My love mixed in the water of my eyes, and a drop settled at the edge of my right eye as an absolution.

Those Last Stanzas

I went about doing my daily chores. There was a bundle of old sheets occupying a precious corner, where I had thought of putting a bonsai plant; the room, it seemed, would do good with a painting, or the little bookshelf, which looked so awkwardly placed, needed a desperate change. I looked around and found hundreds of changes that needed to be made in the room. An impish, punctilious kid in me was always pondering about making those changes, and the next moment the procrastinator in me would come out and prioritise food. And I would go around rummaging for the gorgeous packets on the shelf, always hoarding something nice to mix and prepare a sumptuous meal with. And that was usual, food getting prioritised over everything else in the room.

My heart gave a guffaw…and ignoring the little imp in me, I proceeded to the kitchen. And there were, as always, some chunks of vegetables and a packet of vermicelli to count on, a glass of soya milk with chocolate powder. Too many thoughts occupied my mind, and I drifted from one meaningless distraction to the other. I was too messed up in my head, a storm of thoughts rising in that little space.

As a kid, I used to venture far in our society, and my sister was always handed the task of bringing me back home. I always held a small packet in my pocket, which I would use to keep my small belongings collected from the roadside. My sister knew the trick; she knew well where to find me. I would go far to collect pebbles, and I considered them my talisman.

'This is just a stone, okay, a bit shiny, but still just a stone, and it does not have any magical spells,' she would say. But that stone was my talisman, and I dreamt of chanting some spell and turning the shiny pebbles into beings or flames or beautiful wildflowers. Twenty years later, I realised my search was never over, there were still pebbles to be collected as talismans, spells to be chanted and lives breathed in my collection.

I was again venturing out into the unknown, into the darkness and this time no one was there to find me and bring me back home. I looked at myself and wondered where all the talisman has gone—there was just emptiness around me. Suddenly, I wanted to cry—not those ladylike tears that trickle like pearls on your cheeks, but more like the ones that accompany howling at the moon. I tried to suppress that urge, but my throat was arid, almost paining, and my eyes were wet holding those unshed tears. And then, we had to keep moving, accept the present without reflecting much on the past.

***

It was a hot day at the end of the monsoon. A hot wind blew from time to time, stopped suddenly and returned suddenly, full of dust. I waited for Nikhil to come, almost unsure if he would come. A pencil of feeble sunlight shone coldly on the footpath of the boulevard, that seemed to come from time immemorial and go on till eternity, and looked like an innocuous virgin in the sea of humanity assembled there. I stood in one corner, waiting for his call, waiting to see him, one last time perhaps. How do break-ups even look like, I wondered. That sweet feeling and that innocuous charm of finding someone who you knew could understand you had been ruffled. Now, only the ashes of that feeling remained. And you can't hold onto them. You must let those sands slip off your hands, forget and move on. So hard to even think…love isn't just a part of life, it is life in itself.

He called.

We whisked into an intimate restaurant in Connaught Place. We were meeting after almost two months. His demeanour lacked a display of love, mine looked more calculated, carrying a hint of natural reluctance. It was a tete-a-tete with those eerie dreams, which never waited for the night to draw and lurked with their ghastly claws. I looked at him as I looked at a predicament of loss. I could see my dreams lost in that body, little pieces of theirs staring at me, some mocking me, some laughing, and some weeping. And in those shiny little pieces, I could see all the dreams I had once decorated my life with, turning into loss, taking with them everything I had ever wanted. In that certain moment, I felt lost and the world outside moved, the clock covered its time, the sun and moon chased each other, and the vast sea of people carried their memories and hopes to live a new day, as I sat there, lost, fishing for the remnants of the bright moments from our past.

"Should we get coffee, with soya milk? I know you can never say no to it." His words broke the silence.

"Sure, you know so much about me."

"How have you been?" And yes, we had to talk like strangers before the tumultuous conversation could begin. I wanted to skip the general greetings, scream at him and ask 'why'. I sat there, answering whatever questions he had. I couldn't even pull myself up to answer him with more than a line. My shoulders sagged in defeat as my doubts crept back to me and my loss stared at me.

"Nikhil, what about us?" The words pierced me as I spoke.

"You know, Anuj, some things are meant to die. I am happy that we are breaking up on a good note, and that till we were together, we cared for each other and that we shall always do, wherever we are," he said it—all in one sentence.

I took a deep breath. No more questions were needed to be asked, no more answers to be sought. It was all settled, and all it ever required was one sentence…one sentence to end what had survived for seven years.

It was over. And thankfully, we didn't make a pretence of understanding and empathising. So, what now? Our romance had crawled back to the nothingness it had risen from. Nikhil and I were never friends; we started as lovers and ended as lovers. And with one statement, which I had guessed was coming, we were back on our individual paths, back to being the strangers we were before we were brought together by mutual desires.

There was nothing more to do, our breaking up was as uncomplicated as our coming together had been. It was stupid of me to feel broken when I knew what was coming, but I could feel the silence hanging between us, accompanied by a gnawing absence of compassion.

And after a minute or two of silence, in a low, suppressed tone, I asked him, "Are you with someone else?"

"No, Anuj, I'm not, and not looking to be for some time. You know, I just feel tired. Things were good between us, but probably not good enough to sustain for more time."

"It sustained for seven years." My voice grew heavy and hoarse.

"It's nothing about you, it's the silly me. I probably have a very different idea about life, and that doesn't look possible with you."

"And what is your idea?" I asked.

"I need a simple life, Anuj. Our lives are a mess; half the time we think about how others will react; it's layer after layers of lies. Can you live it forever? You may take me for a coward, someone unwilling to fight for his love, but that is it. I just want it simple."

I felt a rush of rage run through my veins when he said that. I had no idea what he was hinting at even, but yes, I could live that forever, for whatever he was hinting at defined me. "We were never equal partners in this, it was a different affair, and then with distance, things grew, realisation set in, and with that I could easily see how different we two are. We weren't meant to be together, or we were just two good souls who came together and survived the bad times. We were destined to grow apart with time. Didn't you ever think so?"

"And you learnt to live without me, never even attempting to look back and see if I'd be able to cope," I said morosely. A break-up doesn't simply break your heart and leave the pieces for you to put back together; it shreds it into tiny pieces which cannot be joined again. And as you walk through the rubble left behind, you look for these pieces, you want to keep some, however rotten or tainted, as memories. Those pieces haunt you, wake you up in the middle of the night, and make you long for the touch and feel of the love you have lost. Despite the sorrow, you hold onto these pieces.

Can anyone ever forget their first love? I have no answer for it, probably there is no answer, except an explanation that needs to move on. Move on… another heavy word. I realised that the previous day, and I probably had moved on, sewed a new heart and life for myself, and still at that particular moment, with him looking into my eyes and I into his, and our eyes full of questions: my heart sank and I knew there was nothing like a moving on. A part of you is crashed, broken, or lost, and that part is never coming back. The pain is perpetual; it will be slowly rotting inside you most of the time, or become explosive at times. It would heal with time, but the scar is mostly too deep to go away.

"Try to contemplate this, you can't put silver caps on a relationship and think it will live. I started feeling ruffled in our relation. I don't blame you. I think it's with gay relations; things are never just about us, and we keep compromising, looking for easier grounds. Soon, relations start looking like being forced upon you. Maybe I can just ask for and expect to get your forgiveness," he said. His words were honest, and I could get that.

The numbness was beginning to trickle down from head to toe. Like something inside me moving and breaking swiftly. I was perturbed by the situation in hand. I knew it and I had come prepared for it, and a part of me wanted it to be swift, yet my mind was overtaken by that feeling. Something broke inside me, my heart sank, and my senses fazed. At that moment, I knew that one can never prepare oneself to put a relationship aside. It's something one had cared for and nursed.

It seemed that my world had changed in a moment without a clear warning, albeit a warning was always there. I knew it would be foolish of me to even hope of our relationship blossoming back, and at that time I really didn't care. The choice had been made well before the choice came to me.

The bill was paid, and then came time to part. I saw him leave while I remained seated, gathering my thoughts, trying to absorb my loss or just the actualisation of that. There's something within all of us that remains stuck to the walls, the walls our ideas emanate from. It doesn't come off, and we can never get rid of it easily. Losses are not perpetual and wins are ephemeral. We tried everything we possibly could, from alcohol to sex, from fleeting things to repeating gossips, to staying far from even the momentary feeling of loss. Yet it persisted, deep within, in deep slumber, waiting for the opportune moment when it could rise and stare at us and the vast expanse of meaningless in our love life.

We tried it all, still it was never enough. Our love wanted more compromise. It fed on our traumas and trivial pleasures, and with distance, the gaping loss became clearer. And slowly, it turned from nurturer to parasite, feeding on our thoughts and psyche. We were left emotionally depleted. We forgot to breathe, or laugh, or think, or reflect. Our rapid footprints left a trail of our fears, and with every step, the loss became clearer and deeper. We tried enough, and then we realised we were drained of trying.

Some things are meant to die, they live their age, blossom, die and fall like a dead leaf, and they leave a scar, which can only be filled by a new blossom, and the cycle continues. After every loss is a preparation to start again, and it goes on till the time you are completely replenished or completely drained.

I drove around for almost an hour, windows down, air blowing in my face, music as loud as the stereo could allow, trying to block out all my thoughts. Even if you get back something after it has been lost, it never remains the same. I realised that evening, I was not the type who let go of things, but the type who held on to empty words, promises, and hope. I held on so tight to that emptiness and for so long that I forgot who I was and who I wanted to be. I was for him his strongest backbone, the light at the pit of all his darkest moments, and the strong beat to his weak heart. I had always put him first, even after all the hurt.

And there we were, two people who entered the restaurant as once lovers and came out as strangers. I took in a deep, startled breath, parked my car, waited for a moment, walked my way to the coffee shop, and ordered another cup of coffee. The aroma of hot brewing coffee and freshly baked bread was relaxing. And the next moment, I called Dhruv.

"I got my answers. It is officially over. I feel so broken and messed up right now. I am unable to accept the obvious." My voice carried the heaviness of a longing heart.

"Are you still there? What are your plans?" He asked. No questions about the massive loss I had gone through, maybe it was his way—not looking back and putting the focus on the future.

"What plans will I have…I knew it would happen and was damn prepared for it."

"Don't panic, just chill. Send me your location, let me come there for you. And allow me to take you to some serious theatre."

"Your serious theatre means a musical comedy shtick, which I doubt can soothe my heart," I replied, my tone relaxing and my inner goddess coming alive.

"Excuse me," he huffed, "anyone who doesn't think comedy is an art form certainly hasn't read much Shakespeare, have they?" And I could imagine him with hackles raised as he huffed his irritation. And the next fifteen minutes were spent in enlightening me about his 'professional shtick', and he went on to deliver a tart, pedantic lecture on French neo-classics and the cultural impact of the musicals in artistic and oral history.

The shrill diatribe left a puff of hot breath in me, but his enthusiasm was inviting, too. And instead of being completely put off by the snootiness in his voice, I felt like rolling my eyes, giving him an easy smile, putting my arms around him, and whispering in his ears 'I love you'.

"I must admit that didactic spell of yours has pepped me up to go for that theatre." I said with a broad, baritone laugh. Alarm and scepticism warred with spreading unsteady warmth behind my collarbone. I could imagine him smiling at the other end of the phone too. A riveting, pacifying smile.

He was weird, he loved theatres but called literature the last refuge of the tragically uncool. And it was so incredibly easy to jive from one topic to the other in our conversations: from books and theatre to politics and our personal histories. All our old conversations flashed by. One evening and I traversed one end of my love life to the other—an arduous journey, from a consolation of a deadly loneliness that ate into my soul like a malignant tumour to the promises of a new life.

My coffee arrived, a latte of deep promises. On any day, even after a heated argument with Nikhil, I would take time to console my weeping heart. But not that day. That day, I felt free. I felt an uncanny sense of achievement—like I'd broken through something heavy. I wanted to laugh, loud and unfiltered, just from the relief of it all. For the first time in a long while, I felt like I could finally stretch my wings. I had walked away from a relationship that had slowly caged me—one long year of loving without being truly seen, of chasing an illusion and calling it paradise.

I waited, scrolling through the updates on proceedings on Section 377, and as I scrolled through the news items on my phone, many thoughts spun in my mind. It would be historic, a red-letter day in social justice. Love had been criminalised. If passed through, it would be a break from the archaic, demonic ways of relegating a community to margins. I wondered how things could change, might not change much on social terms and the way society is, but it would bring many voices to the mainstream, start an era of dialogue on equality and would see a new brand of advocacy.

It had the potential to create a quake and shake many fundamentals of society. To start with, the alternative would be recognised, a day or two of media and political clamour would bring many voices, thoughts, and ideas to the fore. That's what striking down the section would mean to the nation. But what if the judgment went the other way and the court upheld the status quo? Millions would lose hope. No, that would be a nightmare. But wasn't there a possibility of that? There was, and a high possibility too.

And then the political regime, led by the right-wing actors, was patronised by radical, conservative wings who held majoritarian views and had been vocal against the LGBTQ+ movement. Many political leaders and ideological allies of the ruling party had not taken an official stand on decriminalising same sex relations, similar to the ultra-orthodox of the Americas and Europe. That was the right wing's legitimised stand at the global level. And the politics of the country hadn't shaped up enough to accept LGBTQ+ rights.

Before the judgment, the Indian government had opted to abstain from voting on human rights for LGBTQ+ debate in the United Nations. The political environment where the orthodox, majoritarian views were gaining ground was anything but encouraging. And even if the judgement was passed, how far could the movement go if the society got gripped under a majoritarian, heteronormative narrative?

I made mental notes and decided to write an article pertaining to the judgment. My phone buzzed. *Another five minutes.* I smiled. Even in probably the most heightened times for the community, the roaring tides in my life had settled. The storm in my life was over, and I could imagine myself settling down with Dhruv in the future.

And there he came—in a kurta with an asymmetrical hemline and pleated details, made with linen blend, worn over sneakers and jeans.

"Isn't the corporate strategist looking a darling hunk today?" I teased.

"Well, I can take this as a compliment if this pleases your heart."

I couldn't hold myself from offering an easy smile and a half-hug. "The thing is that we will have to shelve the plan for theatre for some other day. You probably spent a lot more time than required to reconcile with your past." 'Reconcile' seemed a pretty untoward choice of word to put there, but from him everything always sounded mellifluous to me. "The show will start in another half an hour and there are no seats available. So basically, unlike you, some people in Delhi love musicals," he added.

"That's sad. We can go back to my house and I can cook something for you; or we can try something here and then we can go back and I cook something," I stressed.

"Either way, you insist on cooking…" He sounded a bit addled as he said that.

"I desperately need a stress reliever today, and maybe you alone won't do the trick," I said, letting the goddess in me speak.

"And Mr Champagne Socialist, it's just that last time, you made salad, which isn't the pleasing definition of orgasmic." Ahh, and there came a literary barb to pierce my salubrious soul. I laughed off my pain.

"Fine sir, I can get you some spaghetti and kebabs today, but I insist on the vegan part. And make this a pact between us, you will not meddle with my vegan choice."

"No, no, never, a vegan gay is a prize catch. Veganism is the new, hot trend, and I respect that." Well, that was quite easy to settle. I smiled wildly and held his hand, his almost delicate hand.

***

And what a delicious way to spend a Saturday night. I stood beneath the shower, absentmindedly washing myself, contemplating the last couple of hours and how life moved in those hours. From one coffee to the other, my life took a big turn. My subconscious pursed its lips at me and shook its head. A wide smile spread on my face. The promises of a new life stared at me, their loving gaze fixed on my naked body. Dhruv prepared cocktails in the living room. Life seemed so love-worthy.

I wore my casuals and lusted after him in his chic kurtas. Staring at my reflection, I smiled at the memories of the evening, the cancelled plan and the chance to spend another night wrapped in his arms. It had been an immature relationship with Nikhil. I was young, he was young, and we were two different minds brought together by the cruel handiwork of Cupid. Dhruv seemed a guy out of a classy rom-com written just for me. He looked a classic work of Rembrandt, genuine, artsy and deeply enticing. Perhaps it was right of me to think that, with him, it could work.

"Oh, so what is keeping the corporate strategist, cum timeless connoisseur and oenophile, cum lover of a lonely soul, so ardently busy?" I announced, seeing him knee-deep in preparing drinks. He turned and stood immobilised, eyes glimmering and hungry. I blushed crimson everywhere.

"I am trying hard to give an everlasting first impression to my vegan delight," he replied. He looked so wickedly tempting in the wonderfully knit kurta, with his ruffled hair, dark eyes dancing with erotic thoughts, and sexy, amused smile. I smiled, unsure of hiding my desire.

"Well, I must say I feel a little flattered here." A brief smile flitted across my lips. We were talking in short sentences, letting our eyes do most of the talking. Or was there even something to talk about? I had one persistent feeling caught in my heart, and that was to collapse in his arms and feel the warmth of his body. He gazed down at me, his eyes glowing, warm and loving.

"And here it is for my newfound love," he said, offering me the cocktail he had so painstakingly prepared.

"Truly, I feel so weird right now. I broke up with my seven-year-long boyfriend in the evening, and now I am raising a toast with you and starting my new love life."

"Well, feel happy for your situation. I don't even remember how much I had cried or how much time it took me to absorb that pain of losing a love. It took me three years to prepare myself to be with another person," he murmured and I felt a deep regret in my heart for touching that sensitive side of his. And all I could do was to inch closer to him, give him a soft, warm hug and whisper in his ears, "I won't leave you!"

That moment I knew, buried deep within Dhruv was a deeply emotional and fragile person, a soul that lived for love. And I loved to look into the richly decorated, emotional side of his. He was a lovely creature, inspiring a sea of emotions in me—true and gentle.

"Sorry to ask, but don't you think it will get difficult when people get to know about us at work," I muttered in an unassuming tone, probably a wrong question.

"Let's resist from playing it out in front of the office. See, I am not even out to my family or the world, as I feel one's orientation is deeply personal to one and not a grand affair about which everyone needs to know. And so I never thought of opening up. But it's just me, and it's also I never had a relationship that I had to take to a certain end, to talk about. When I have and I wish to make it a permanent affair, I won't shy away from opening to the world." He rolled his eyes at me as he said the last sentence, and my inner goddess swooned and jumped with delight.

"Well, I wasn't pointing to that, I was just trying to suggest to keep a little distance at the office. You know, I hate unnecessary gossip or probably I am mentally not quite prepared for it." I expressed the brewing storm in my head. He smiled back.

"We won't, also because I am still to settle in the place and know people, I'm sure I can't afford an avoidable controversy."

"So happy we both agree that we need to keep it low," I said with a comfortable smile spreading on my face, "but that doesn't mean we keep it low here." The naughty me spoke and took a step towards him to engage in a feather-soft kiss.

"That's insane," he huffed.

"I am entitled to such insanity when you are around."

I smiled a reassuring smile and said, "I'll make dinner and after that, I need to fashion you into my vessel." The large, chocolate eyes in my piquant little face gleamed.

"And may I ask the chef—what's on the menu today?" He replied in an equally tingling manner, changing the course of the conversation, finding it too difficult to handle and too futile to continue.

I couldn't help but smile, I had always loved this trait in him. He could so easily bring himself out of one conversation and shift to another, and for feelings, they were too sacred to be spent when not wanted.

"Let me check the impressive refrigerator we have and let's see if I can mix up some stuff and create some culinary magic," I said in a chirpy tone. The old grief seemed to have evaporated for some time, albeit leaving a stink.

Perhaps cooking a troubled man's dinner was a better idea than letting him sink in your arguments and dig the inner meaning. I opened the fridge and peered inside—nothing impressive. A meal with two tomatoes, a handful of droopy beans and some sick capsicum, was not possible; poor soul, he would have to manage with a regular spaghetti.

"Hey, should I do a mouth-watcring spaghetti for you? I know the health freak inside you deserves something nutrient rich but there isn't anything here," I said in an indulgent way, expecting a loud war cry from him. Oh! No reply, that was just too cruel for a chirpy me to be left unattended and unanswered. Well, sometimes silence is a bitter ointment between couples and an easy way to bring things to normal.

I was humming under my breath as I came out and asked, "You didn't like the idea?"

"Oh, I believe if a man isn't saying a thing, it is taken as a 'yes.'" He sounded positively put off. "Hey, by the way, did you check the shelves, last time I saw some soyabean nuggets and olives at the back of the cupboard. You can make something with soya, will be better than spaghetti," he said enthusiastically, implicitly patronising his choice. His statement left me a little surprised; he had come to know my house so well.

"Now that's a cooler combination, give me some time to prepare something refreshing and spread the lavish table around," I said, smiling in an attempt to charm him.

"And you know sometimes we can do better than refreshing spaghetti with olives, and salads with exotic fruits, we can try some soulful, to the definition junk and dirty foods," he said crossly.

"Oh, so someone finds the vegan choices cagey…I concur, but only some days. As for dirty, let's hold that word for the bed," I winked as I spoke.

"For the bed…that sounds too cheesy. I am in the mood for something more thrilling," he rolled his eyes, trying to breeze off his frustration with my salad ways.

I put a pot of water on the boil as I chopped the vegetables. Though the kitchen was poorly stocked, the lavishly designed kitchen had never failed to put me in a celebrity chef mode.

"In the kitchen, you are quite a little Tarla Dalal," Dhruv quipped, appearing suddenly at the door. He could move in as silently as a panther employing his old jungle tricks.

"And sir, no disturbance…this is my territory," I replied. "And if I don't get you good food, we will miss out on the good sex." Now that was the sensitive spot to strike on.

"At least allow me to stand here and watch you cook."

I put the potatoes to boil in a cooker, the spices were waiting to be added, and the onion-garlic paste was getting readied in the grinder.

"May I help you?"

"Well, to be candid, I am rather enjoying this. And do remind me to send a personal note for this flirtatious smile, which has been set on your sweet face since evening," I murmured, my inner goddess jiving with pleasure. "And well, if you really want to help, you can help me with the rice. Pour off the water from this vessel; there's rice in that bowl; add some water, sprinkle salt, and then put that in the microwave to cook. Set it to fifteen minutes. By that time, I will have the curry sorted out. I shall fritter the soyabean over the curry, hope that works." He behaved the way a good lover should.

"And once this is done, I need a good kiss," he murmured, nibbling gently at the nape of my neck. I smiled in pleasure.

"You will." I turned around to face him, lifting my head to drop a kiss on his lips.

***

Dhruv sighed and shifted reluctantly, dragging the quilt to lie beside me, crossing his thigh over mine and his head on my elbow. He gazed at me, a warm, comforting look. He had come a long way, and so had I—a life of questions and assurances. He came as a new beginning to me. It was too much to be absorbed in moments, and with too much happening in my life, it seemed I had lost sight of that simple, honest transition. But that night, I wished to absorb the gentility of those moments. Those gentle stares, genuine giggles, the concern shown from time to time, that ability to connect and feel for each other, the numerous moments that brought us together.

He held me by my waist and came closer to kiss me. I could see honesty in his dark eyes. I let my eyes roam over his body. His bronze skin was glowing under the moonlight, and his dark brown eyes sparkled. He looked more beautiful up close, his high, straight nose shone beatifically.

"I will never get enough of you," he murmured and kissed me, his tongue relentlessly needy. I moaned in deep pleasure and clasped his dear, dear face. His hand fondled my neck behind.

"Same here...you know, you are my best therapy," I breathed, inching closer to him so that our noses touched.

He clasped my face in his hands and rubbed his thumb over the tips of my fingers in an urge to take me in his embrace once again. And I was ready to be his; my eyes refused to leave him. I ran my finger over his body; I wanted to cry and fight against all the powers of this earth to be his, to remain in his arms. I closed my eyes, took a deep breath, and pinned my body against his to enjoy the delicious friction as he rubbed his hands all over me. I buried my hands in his hair and, bending my face against his, consumed him in a passionate kiss, my tongue as covetous as his. I wanted to live him fully. A dark breath of impatience struck me as I closed my eyes, and I pulled myself harder to him. He was a splendid lover, as positive and as ardent and as vocal in his cries of delight as I was.

My hooded eyes looked deep into his, and a slow smile came across my face, sweet at first and then broader and deeper until it grew mesmerising. I was flushed with joy and contention. My heart was pounding. Everything had happened so quickly that it left a part of me bewildered and bewitched. The other part was dancing with drunk madness. I deeply wanted him to assure me. He looked at me and locked me in an unforgettable kiss.

"I will always be there for you," he said and kissed my forehead, trailing down to the back of my neck to my chest, then to my belly. I enjoyed as his tongue trailed my body. I was right, losing myself to him was so intoxicating. All worries obliterated—I was there with him, my blood singing in my veins, thrumming loudly as I moaned and reacted to his actions. The music of his kisses was artfully getting mixed with my panting breaths.

"Slowly..." I breathed. "I want to feel you inside me," I murmured, getting dissipated with his brisk rhythm, wanting him more.

In reply, he kissed me gently, bit my lip, and absorbed my moans.

I buried my hands in his soft, gelled hair and surrendered myself to his rhythm; the blood in my veins soaring higher and then plateauing and then falling hard and fast, matching the fervour of his pace. I dug my nails hard into his skin and called out his name; his name a benediction on my lips, releasing me of all my qualms.

I pushed him on the bed and started kneading and squeezing his hard belly muscles. Those small moments were essential for me, and I wanted to bask in the serene afterglow of our love-making. He rested his head close to mine, his arms wrapped around me, his fingers foraging into my hair, and he smiled a comfortable smile, and I involuntarily tilted to face him.

"I love you," he murmured softly in my ears. His voice was so tantalisingly good.

The D-Day Is Coming

For two days, we were together. We let no thoughts pass us, except for those where we were together. And as night smudged into light, and wrong smudged into right, we smudged into each other. Feeling extreme freedom, we locked ourselves in each other's embrace, losing ourselves as we made tireless attempts to win over each other, and forgetting the sight of an end as we inched towards a new beginning. There had not been a better Monday morning in a long time than that one, waking in his arms with a smile spread like a thin film of ornaments on my face, caressing my soul.

He woke up and like a little baby, rubbed his eyes. I couldn't stop myself from smiling, a carefree smile, reflective of the happiness within.

"Should I don the responsibility of making coffee every morning?" And there you go, how can you not love a person who can whip some cream and make you a deeply invigorating coffee? "You need a strong one to stir the chaos in your mind."

"Oh, I am sure someone walked into my life and clouded all my thoughts. I can manage with a little chaos…"

I saw him stir sugar in my coffee. I watched the sweetness dissolve — not vanish, but surrender as though it ached to become something greater than itself. It died gently, slipping into something purer. I had stirred my own chaos the same way, over and over, until there was nothing left to rise above or fall beneath. Just stillness. My inner goddess laughed, like there was no before or after and everything had condescended to the present. It must have been a loud guffaw, just that there was no noise. A kind of cosmic mirth.

I wore a prosaic smile, stating loudly how beautiful life could be with him around.

He brought me my coffee with some oat cookies and a deeply satisfying smile. In two days, my life had slowed down, and I had never loved it more. It was the start of a new love, at a new age, with a new me, and it was magical. I wondered why I had caught myself up in the pace of things when a gradual slowing down of life was all I ever wanted. We all want that, life to be slow, and being able to see and live the beauty of every moment.

"And here's your coffee," he said, offering me my cup and taking a seat next to me on the couch.

"Hasn't this all happened too quick?" I said coyly.

"Quick, but I think we gave ourselves good time yesterday, and as I told you, I like it slow."

"Oh, not the sex part," I brushed him off for being mistaken, "I was talking about the whole thing between us, it's just been a month for you to join the office, and here we are waking up together."

"You are sounding as if you regret this," he teased. I chose to giggle cheekily and take that chance to snuggle up to him.

"Sorry for even putting forth that glut of an idea. The fact is that I am bombilating with anticipation and hope," I whispered, still in awe.

"Keep that hope brimming till evening. Let's go for dinner today, I know a good fusion restaurant," he lured me again with his contagious smile.

"Let's go for something more authentic, any cuisine. The ungainly fact is that accidentally, whatever I make at home is a version of fusion food." I had no idea I was trying to compliment myself for the numerous culinary experiments I did from time to time, or flaringly mocking myself. I looked at him for a reaction.

"A good Vietnamese then."

I ran a finger down his chest and cheekily answered, "Great; sounds like something to inspire my palate."

The leisurely pace with which we had our coffee, and the young and cheerful laughs, radiating joyful elation, had me thinking if he was in a mood to spend another day. I could join his plan of staying away from work and spend the entire day doing nothing but being locked in his arms. I grabbed his hands to hold on, feeling his muscles ripple, and rested my head on his shoulders. He laughed. And his infectious laughter swept me off—dizzy, addled and totally smitten by him. He looked at me, clasped my face with his hands and kissed me. Hard. His tongue insisting, persuasive and inciting.

"If you continue working your magic on me, I don't think we are going to work today. It's not right to keep a man off his work and engaged in something so beautiful," and he came down and kissed me again. And as our tongues rolled, a storm brewed inside me and a dark breath of fear swept me. I closed my eyes. That wasn't the time for my fears and insecurities to come to the surface and let these thoughts cast their shadow on my splendid present. I wanted to float, and I wanted to float in desire. His lips parted, only to lock my lips again. We kissed and smiled, and smiled and kissed.

***

The real test, however, was to maintain distance in the office and to give an impression that nothing existed between us. Dhruv left early, basically after coffee. And I took my time to reach office; walking the same diminutive paths, the images remained the same, but the accompanying thoughts had changed from sullen to salacious. It would be wrong to say that his were the only thoughts surfacing in my mind. There was a lot that was churning and ready to break free. It was just three days to the judgement that could change lives of millions like me. Every hour passed like a lifetime. A freedom so close, and still so far.

Dhruv had entrusted me with shows every evening to come out openly in support of the judgement, and he knew the support had to be built. A lot could and would change if the law was passed and homosexual relations decriminalised. India stood on the cusp of a change, and millions like me waited in their decorated shells for the judgement. It would be a coming-out moment for many. The day would be marked with tears, and smiles, and hopes, and promises. Lives would be lived in those moments. It would be a never-before moment, another freedom for millions, a freedom to be who they are, to accept themselves, to not be looked at as criminals, freedom of choice, to love, to live their identity, and above all, a notional freedom from the chains of fears, insecurities and vulnerabilities.

I reached office. The junior scriptwriters had prepared my script for the evening. My team knew me. They knew how attached I was to the program. The program had proven a window for many to put forth their feelings. It lived on those stories. I looked for Dhruv in his cabin. He was there. I waved at him and he waved back, a bit reluctantly. Hesitancy and uncertainty emerged at once as the joint keynotes of his character, unless he was shy and doing his bit to conceal the real person. But discovering the real Dhruv, that too in that setup, was no easy task.

Dhruv usually kept his thoughts to himself and it was hard to gauge what was going on in his mind. He opened up slowly, deliberately, and only to those he trusted.The rhythm was often halting, unsure, but one that softened with time. He observed, contemplated, and would take his time to loosen the grip. And then the glimpses of the person beneath would begin to flicker through. But that hesitancy could be to keep himself concealed and guarded from others.

I, for myself, deeply abhorred the idea of maintaining that sacred veil of secrecy.

I took the script to read, and after making some notes and changes, I paced to Dhruv's room. "I am not sure what to say, it's just that I wanted to see you. And so I thought I could run you through the changes I believe are required in the script." A sense of uncertainty hung in my voice.

He gave me a furtive smile. Got it, it was a calculated way to discourage further attempts. Seeing the spirit so suddenly established in the conversation beginning to fade, I returned to the old tone. "I am not sure what more I can do now, or is the script capturing the real essence of the voices we hope to represent."

"You know you can come here without an excuse." A simple statement to nail down the irrelevance of my action. I felt embarrassed in love, or was there more humour in him than met the eye? "You know my thought on engagement in the show is that every time you speak something, you leave a question to be answered, and with that, you try to open layers, argument by argument, statement by statement, or just say, story by story."

"Keeping myself to the minimum, you suggest?"

"Well as I see it, you don't own the place. It's our listeners who have gathered courage to share their stories, who own it. Let them laugh, cry, share the intimate details, argue, feel cheated or feel angry or relaxed—but make your show all about their voice." He looked at me with an ardent, atmospheric gaze. And then he blinked, carrying a degree of hesitancy in his eyes.

"I get it." I smiled, appreciative of his words.

"Do you want to come to my home today after office and discuss it more? I am certain we can reflect on this more." Dhruv asked.

"Sure. And because this week is so important, and in a way even a thought of that is freezing me out, I will be happy to spend more time with you and relax my mind," I said, looking at him. No, that wasn't out of love, that was a necessity, I wanted to keep my focus intact. I had a volcano of emotions inside me waiting to explode, and I needed his company to keep this energy contained within or directed wisely.

"You know I will always be there when you need me."

"In the little time that I have known you and you have known me, I can say that you don't have to say or I ask these things. This is to be understood and it's quite clear. I shall be at your home after finishing my show, and damn, I will judge you on your hospitality," I chuckled. He smiled, and with that I took his leave.

I logged onto my Twitter and checked the latest tweets on the Section 377 hearing. The support was overwhelming. And as India prepared to take a move towards a more liberal society, the youth of the country took the front. The social media brimmed with unseen positivity, the centuries-old hatred and injustice were swept away by enthusiasm and hope. But it was a decades-old battle, a colonial-age law that suppressed the sexual choices of millions and compelled people to live dual lives. Discrimination won't go with one stroke of the pen, it was the weight of years of injustice and intolerance that had kept people locked in their shells and not come out of the closet and embrace their truths. Support was needed from all sections of society. It was more than Twitter hashtags and newspaper articles; the society had to get acquainted to and develop appreciation with the idea.

***

Evening was harder to handle. I felt burdened under the weight of my conscience. There were stories, and with the stories I got acquainted to the feelings of self-guilt, of invisible glass ceilings, insecurity of relationships, agony, pain, betrayal, and the feeling of discrimination and indifference.

"I have no idea why I did that, but I felt emotionally broken. My entire life seemed a lie, like I was living under some kind of a veil. On the face of it, the media industry seems to be really liberal and queer friendly, but there are still corners of the industry that are not diverse in any respect," a forty-year-old Anand started telling me his story. He continued, "That can feel isolating and more…like you're on the outside of a club that you'll never be a member of. And you are outside for no fault of yours..."

"Were you out to everyone, Anand, or how did you sense this prevailing homophobia in your office space?" I asked, doing exactly as Dhruv had told me, letting people speak their hearts.

"You can't say it was homophobia or indifference, there is no formula to it. But you know when it happens, you can feel being left out. You can never make it to those informal clubs where all the decisions happen, and then you know you are stuck. It is never overt, no one teases you, mocks you for who you are, or judges you for the way you talk, the movies you watch, or the clothes you wear—you are just...kind of... ostracised. This prejudice flows deep and remains hidden. There is a lack of emotional intelligence in the corporate world sometimes. And it's poorer for us."

The way he stressed 'us' took me by surprise. I couldn't help but ponder moments where I felt a hint of this indifference, and he said it's never to your face, it just floats within the surface, like an invisible tide always rearing its head to strike you. The general feeling in any workplace is that there are always certain undefined boundaries to which you can get personal with someone, or share your personal life, and there are limits to which you can foresee how a colleague would react, and you can never ascertain if the relations and bonds you forge are real or just forced upon and lived in the name of professionalism. There aren't easy answers in this finely crafted world.

"It took me a long time to accept my sexual identity. I often wondered if it's just a phase, or if it happens to many. In the beginning, it was even difficult to come to terms with it. It was different, and in many ways, I felt it was wrong. I tried getting on hetero relations, you know, just to be like other guys in my group, but then I realised the emotional laziness and the weight associated with such forced associations," Daniel confessed. He chose to talk with me frankly and himself out to the world.

"When did you realise this, Daniel, and tell me how you felt? And tell me, how does it feel opening yourself up to the world?" I asked.

"It took me time, but eventually, I managed to put a name to my malaise: homosexuality. And the realisation came in one unsuspecting event, on a bus, when a boy put his hand on my thigh. I suddenly froze. I didn't know what to do. As soon as the bus stopped, I fled. But that evening, I was obsessed with the thought of that trivial gesture. I thought about it consistently and how badly I wanted that. That thought occupied my mind, not letting it sleep. The touch by a boy seemed terribly good, and I hoped it would happen again. That probably was my moment of reckoning, when in all likelihood, someone tried to violate me. But he made me realise what was burning me from inside. I gradually discovered and accepted my sexuality…"

As he went on, pouring his heart out, he kept on losing the pace of his tone. And with his stories came out the years of uncertainty and insecurity buried deep within him. In that act, he freed himself. I gave him time. I could hear his voice break, and I could imagine his eyes full of tears. It was courageous of him, coming out to the world, and in that journey, coming out to oneself, embracing the deepest secrets of oneself. Those were moments of sincere vocation.

"I reflected on my life and tried to decode it. I could get the hidden meaning of the several passes made out at me in the college, and recounted moments when I was subjected to sustained emotional solicitations and recurrent flirtations." His tone got nostalgic, and he sounded deeply agonised as if an emotional storm was on its way to hit him, and he could clearly see the eye of the storm. It was deep in his college days.

He continued, "I guess I never realized that just trying to be discreet about my choices could actually *invite* trouble. I was a bit naïve to open up to a friend. What I didn't know was that he would betray me and tell everyone around him. When you live in a closed society that can't handle anything outside the norm, you never really know who's on your side or how they'll show up. It's all grey. Straight folks usually don't get it. Or they judge it before they even try." Each syllable of his sentence was distinct; I could sense the lava inside him waiting to explode.

"It's okay, Daniel. I am sure our listeners can get from your story how challenging being a queer is in our society. We all lead difficult lives. We go through a lot, and we are expected to hold those stories within us. And this is our show, where you can tell your stories, put forth your questions, and be assured that you will not be judged," I said, trying to assuage him, though on the inside, I wanted the lava to come out and for him to declare the emotional turmoil within.

"I was violated," he declared the next instant, his confession coming as a bolt from the blue. "They were three, I was beaten and then violated, and I couldn't do a thing. There was no one I could tell, no friends, family or anyone else. I couldn't even tell the doctor who treated me. All because I was gay and they wanted to teach me a lesson. For fifteen years, I have been carrying that weight, that relentless pain, and that's how lonely and tired I am." Daniel broke down, and for a moment there were no words, only sobs. I wished it was not a Radio Show and I could just go and hug him, maybe console him if I could.

"I sometimes wish I were never born this way. I could live my life like normal people, have a family, then kids, and grow old.

I have nothing to look forward to, and there's a dark past which chases me."

I felt devastated, tears ran down my cheeks. On the other side, I could hear him sob. A shrill silence was set, and I had no words or courage to take the conversation forward. I looked at Dhruv through the window and then to the others. All looked like broken souls, not prepared to take this shock. The show, running for now three months, had helped bring out many stories of pain and misery, but this was a dark secret buried in the past, and yet I felt listeners needed to be haunted by reality this way.

His confession took me back to my moment of coming out—of choosing candour over coy. I was reluctant at first, I didn't want to embrace a label that came with so much baggage. But something in me prodded me to face the truth. I came out quite early in life and probably took it on the chin. But I'd never worried about coming out. I felt caged, and the truth was getting too onerous for me. I realised accepting and appreciating your identity was not that easy. You had to unlearn all that you had always been taught, you had seen or heard. It's a big transition.

But however long it takes one to come to terms with oneself, it's never time wasted. Some people just have a longer stretch to walk. Years of pretending to be someone else or living a lie constantly; builds an armour over our skin. It hides the reality but doesn't help.

As queer people, we often don't grow up as ourselves; we grow up playing a version of ourselves that sacrifices authenticity to minimise humiliation and prejudice. We live life in bits, surrounded by more questions than answers. And a massive part of our lives goes in finding answers to those questions; childhood is wasted in actualisation of oneself, adult life goes in un-picking which parts of ourselves are truly us and which parts we have created to protect ourselves, and then a massive part goes in expecting others to understand that we are more than our identity.

As a kid who grew up in a deeply religious, socially committed, and conformist family, coming out as gay was a battle for me. I lived those horrid moments in my mind for years, when my father told me of being ashamed of me, my mother helpless or equally ashamed as he abused me for being who I was. From accepting I was gay to telling the world that I was, I lived my life with hundreds of questions sealed on my lips. And I lived with a constant fear of being a minority in the conformist, majoritarian world around me. I was scared to know that I scare people, my identity scares them, the way I look, eat or think scares them. I scare them because I do things differently than them, or maybe I live differently, think differently, or just that I think. It builds up hate inside them.

"Daniel, how are you feeling?" I asked in a calibrated tone.

"I am. I feel better now. Thank you, thank you for listening to my story" Daniel said in broken words I could imagine the assurance on his face.

"Why are they so afraid of us," Daniel asked quietly, "that it makes them want to break us down?

"Honestly," I said, "I don't think there's a single right answer. Maybe it's fear — some deep-rooted discomfort with anything that doesn't fit the mold. Maybe it's just a reluctance to accept the unfamiliar. Our brains aren't really wired to welcome the alternative. Or maybe," I added with a shrug, "the answer is simpler than all that. Maybe it's not about minds or psychology at all. Maybe people just… choose to be cruel."

I took a breath and added. "I see it as a social dimension too – a battle of minority and majority. The minority is always seen as a threat — not because it actually is, but because the majority *believes* it might shake up the existing order or norms. And no threat is ever just imagined; it's built, piece by piece, then spoon-fed into people with that tired old fear: *what if the minority becomes the majority?* But the minority never becomes the majority — not in any real-world scenario. But that is too logical to be even debated."

"Is it so difficult to tell people that no one is a threat, all we need is equality?" Daniel responded to my reply. At that moment I wondered how his story had opened so many questions that needed an answer — and how this went beyond just queer lives and relations.

"Honestly Daniel, I don't believe in that chorus of everyone's equal. No — that's not the point. A homosexual doesn't necessarily want to be 'equal' to a heterosexual. It's not about wanting *sameness* — it's about being allowed to exist without being framed as a threat." I answered, uncertain of my words even as I spoke them — but somehow, still convinced they held some truth.

I never felt it's about equality. The fundamental thing we desire is appreciation of differences and the realisation that being different doesn't mean harm to their order. The liberal hysteria proclaims it's emancipating the minority, when the minorities never asked for that. All the minority wanted was the majority to accept that we look and act and think differently and have faults of our own. All the minority wants is to live in their perfections and faults peacefully, and with it the gradual redundancy of the word 'minority'—with that comes equality. So, perhaps the battle starts with appreciation of the differences, and the acknowledgement that being different is not being wrong.

Two long hours and I resigned. I came out of the room, exhausted and pained. I was tired, and looked around to catch a glance of Dhruv, who held a content smile on his face. I wished to run and take refuge in his arms, but then it wasn't possible in the office. I took an eyeful of him, while some colleagues inched forward to congratulate me. There was still a day to go for the verdict and my hopes hung by a thread.

The Queerness of the Night

I wanted to do something…write or draw or just make love…but it was so comfortable just to lay there on the bed, with my shoes off, and think—think of everything. I wanted to think of my disconnected thoughts, global affairs, political reshaping in the country, the stories I listened to and, in general, wonder how life had been. Dhruv prepared some food for me, he knew I needed solace and he gave me that space. I sat there motionless, lost, my eyes fixed on the ceiling, a feeling of loss growing inside me.

I wish I could do something, something to distract me from the bubbles floating in my mind. I wondered at the strangeness of things…I remembered how I came out to my sister, her frozen reactions, and how my mother thought that sleeping with a girl would set things right. Right, why was I wrong, how was I wrong, I was born that way—biologically, psychologically and socially 'that' way, the way they thought could be set right.

Something cried in me, screamed in pain, and I felt vanquished, and yet there was no tear, no sob, not a hint of sorrow. There was silence, silence of the dead night. When Daniel was violated by three men, his cries were lost in the silence of the dark night, he was violated for what he was, hated for being who he was. Just like my mother had said 'it will be set right', or my sister had frozen when I came out to her. Was that concern for me, or hate for who I was born as, or just the fear of an alternate idea? Why as society we are so scared of things other than how we have seen things all our life? Thoughts brought thoughts, and as I dug deeper into my past, the pitch-dark memories of the trauma I had to bear came in front of me, like some apparition, enthused to claim the darkness in me and fill it with sadness.

Those silent stares from classmates, those jokes on my feminine ways, the jokes on the way I waved my hand or rolled my eyes, those cues from sex thirsty guys who probably thought I could give them a good time, those concerned but piercing 'no matter who you are' or 'it's all right'—it all came back like nightmares, like some dark, impish thing crawling under my skin, feeding on me and my vulnerabilities. I closed my eyes under the weight of those thoughts. Tears rolled down my cheeks.

I ran down to the other room where Dhruv rested on a couch. I embraced him with passion. "Don't say anything, just let me be like this," I murmured. I needed him alongside me as I pictured myself fighting. I always needed someone.

A slender lamp glowed softly in the room. He turned it down—down to where only a flicker of light filtered through the beaded curtain, diffusing, blurring the image of his handsomeness. And he hugged me tightly, rested his head on mine and planted a kiss on my forehead.

"I think you are taking it too much on yourself. It's sad, it hurts, but it is beyond us to control or set things right. We can just play our roles, and we are doing that," he said in a consoling tone, still holding me tight. "It hurts, but don't keep thinking and wondering about it—that would bring trouble."

I looked at him with large, wet eyes and a careworn smile on my face.

"Should I make you something, a coffee or a drink?" He asked.

I caught the insouciant grin on his face. His heart too had melted after hearing the story, but he wore a breezy look to keep me comforted. He was vexed too, but was able to hide his emotions, and I felt splintered into pieces. Some truths are hard to fathom.

"Sure, whichever you prefer."

"I will go for coffee, but you will have to make an exception for milk today. I will bear in mind to keep a carton of soymilk next time," and he gave me an innocuous smile. I nodded and decided to join him in the kitchen.

"You think I took it way too seriously," I asked him.

"It's fine. We all respond in different ways. There is no set rules that we need to follow. Just be cool. We need our heart and mind in the right place to make decisions." I looked at him, holding a deep gaze, and then he continued, "People, in general, are not taught the ideas of acceptance and tolerance. They grow with ignorance, indifference, and sometimes hate within them. With sexual minorities, it's a hideous mix of all three. And all we can do is to live through those fears."

"I know, the Orlando gay shooting—there is a lot of indescribable hate for our community in this world. Sometimes this hate is violent, at other times, it's just ignoring the existence." I sighed.

"Yeah, I know. It's everywhere. I've come face to face with it in Europe, which has better records of acceptance. India needs time, maybe a lot." He added.

"I feel it's the politics that is vicious, we need compassionate political orders, who can listen and empathise, that can bring in tolerance in the society. That compassionate politics is missing." I looked at him as he talked, and through his words I looked at his compassionate soul.

"You can't lose yourself for these crimes, you are empathetic, turn that empathy into some action. Probably think and put things right. There's a lot of evil in this world, it affects all of us, it has happened to all of us. And not just us, think about others, we all have suffered," he said, a deep sigh in his tone.

"What's the worst that happened to you?" I asked abruptly, looking deep into his eyes, trying to read the inner demons that haunted my man.

He looked back at me, held my hands in deep concern and answered in a deep, anguished voice, "I was violated as a kid."

I lost colour in my face, my hands shook and lips trembled. He had opened me to the darkest and deepest secrets of his life. "I am a survivor, I just feel so lucky about that," he added, eyes wide with fear.

I said nothing, I chose to not say anything, assuming he would say more when he felt free to share.

"Just have your coffee, we will talk about this some other time. Just remember, only a handful knows this truth, I need a lot of trust on someone to even mention that."

"Sure, but you know, you can…" And he put a finger on my lips, and a soft smile on his face said that there was no need for me to say that, he could feel it. I looked at him, attempting to allow something coherent to escape from my lips.

"Just don't talk about that, I will tell you when the time is out, and I have found the strength to tell you. Relations are built on truth, and I won't deprive you of my truth." His aversion was held in check, his jaw was strained and there was tension around his eyes. The truth he gave me was heady, but I was tempered by the fact that he had to undergo such pain as a child, and it is hard to imagine this hideous desecration of some innocuous, young soul. What sort of a monster would violate a child? What sort of a monster would violate anybody?

And I felt that my pain had been replaced by another, it's just the location that had changed, the intensity remained the same, or had rather increased. Perhaps the only sense of relief was that here I could do something. I could just look at him and the heaviness hung in his eyes, my silent stare said: 'With you I shall laugh, for you I shall weep.' I gave him a reluctant smile, a clear signal to drop the topic there and get back to our normal lives.

"I have made some pasta for us. For dinner we can order something," he said.

I wanted to fight the overwhelming need to kiss him and stop the tears pooling in my eyes. I couldn't. And I inched forward to kiss him. His proximity was alluring. He guided my hands up to the curves of his shoulders, so that we were wrapped in each other's embrace. I wanted it. I wanted to hold him and be able to drink all his tears, heal his scars and leave pools of unblemished joy in his life.

I felt his body was painted with bruises and scars that he was forced to hide from the world's blazing eyes of curiosity. Some truths are best hidden from the light of the world, they become clear in darkness.

Our lips parted, with a promising smile that declared our oneness spread on our faces.

"Coffee will get cold," he said.

"It can be heated again, but I can't miss out on the warmth you offer me," I answered, trying to inject some drama in our conversation.

"Is it too early to ask you to shift in with me?" He asked, an amused look set on his face. I flushed red with happiness.

"As happy as I can be that you asked me, I believe it's bit too early for you to consider that. It's not even been a week," I replied, unsure of myself.

"Only if time could define the intensity of a relationship. But then I leave the thought with you, and hope we can try to be together as much as possible."

"Surely," I said, taking a sip of that wonderfully brewed coffee. Well, the naughty part of me just wanted to accept the offer for the coffee he brewed, but the sober part of me wanted to hold on—not getting too deep, too early.

Some More Rainbowed

The next evening, the tension heightened. Just a few hours from the verdict. The show was also going to be hard on me. I had to talk to a transwoman. Transsexuality is the least understood concept in the entire spectrum of queer community. It was hard for me too, and I knew I couldn't use the same brush to empathise with my listener.

"I wish our bodies came with instructions, or a manual for people to understand that we are more than objects of their curiosity," Ray thundered as she spoke to me. I listened ardently. I wanted her to put her story forth; to gain more insights, I had a pre-talk with her before the show started. I didn't want to be startled like the day before, and also, I wanted to be better prepared with her, as in the show, we were going to touch upon a sensitive issue.

"I can understand, Ray, how difficult it is to be a trans, like caught in a different body—"

But before I could say any further, she added, "No, it's more. Like you are always an object of either someone's sexual fantasy, someone's curiosity, or just an object unknown. You are someone to be feared, someone to be belittled, or someone who craves for sympathy—you are never a normal being. There is always a label attached to you. With different people, this label comes with different tags," she blasted. And in the initial two minutes, I could get that the show would be both enraging and engaging.

"Ray, why don't we start from the beginning. Why don't you tell us something about yourself, so that our listeners understand you better" I attempted to quell the rage and set an order to the contrite discourse.

"I was designated male at birth, but I was always a woman inside. You know, as kid I used to secretly dress up in my mother's clothes. You know even consciousness is not fast enough to understand this turmoil of emotions inside. It's like you are in a different body, and except for yourself no one else can know that. As kid or even while growing up, even you don't understand it. And then you start doubting it after you reach a certain age. Like questioning yourself, at times, if everything is fine. There was no one to talk to, Anuj, like no one I could open to, and share what I was going through. My parents always took it as some temporary situation, that stays with kids, and goes away as kids grow old. Just that in my case, these feelings were permanent. You panic because you know there is no way out, just like there is no way back. Not everybody wants it, a struggle with their identity and an inner conflict. I took my time to understand it, and when I did, I made peace with it," she said, a tad riled.

"And do you have any expectations from the verdict, Ray?" I asked, still trying to set the course of conversation, rather leading it.

"I am not sure. Aren't we all used to such assurances. It is so ingrained in the society; it will be difficult for a random ruling to come and change the status quo. You know as trans people we must go around with proof of their identity. We depend on state authorities who would identify them as trans. We have to even struggle to be who we are. Is that not undermining the dignity of a person's identity? I don't think anything will change unless people understand the turmoil that members of the community go through," she said in a balanced tone.

She wasn't wrong. Our society is heavily invested in the idea of gender binaries, the ancient model that divides us into 'two' distinct sexes.

"Ray, if I am not overstepping here into your personal life; how have been your personal experiences and what shaped these? Was it some commonplace prejudice, acts of discrimination or just plain unawareness and indifference?"

"Frankly, it's been a mix of the three. The society doesn't give us many choices. I have been trolled in public, even called out for my identity on social media. And even if the laws come to protect us, how do we voice our identities and positions of gender fluidity to those who do not want to understand or are even not ready to listen? It is suffocating being on the other side, it's uneasy and uncomfortable, and a feeling of being lost and depressed is always around. It's not easy, and you can't pin it down to one reason."

"And what hurts the most is that you never know how the other person sees you—are you being targeted, reduced to gossip, or just seen as someone who can fulfil their wildest sexual fantasies—you have no idea of that. All you know is that your presence evokes a reaction in people." She sighed, almost losing the rage and depth in her voice. Her voice was now heavy, with equal tones of pain, unease and shame.

I didn't think I wanted to know more, not because I wasn't curious, but I felt that sometimes it's just apt to let things remain at the surface. I knew many voices needed an outlet and desired an audience. The society needs to change to accommodate these voices. There are many Rays, Daniels, and Anands around us—more unheard than heard. I alone could not be the agent to bring those voices to fore; there had to be numerous mediums from where these cries can shriek, till there are no cries left to be heard.

I finished my evening shows with two more stories of coming out of the closet. One was about betrayal and a lonely life that followed, and one about family that came out supportive. I was glad I could finish the day on a happy note. I was all laughs and gags as Deb told his story of a supportive family who stood by him as he took decisions of his life, which included moving in with his partner. And as he spoke, he gave me 'couple goals'.

"Hey Deb, I must say you are giving millions of our listeners 'couple goals'..." I said, my hands waving in the air, a soft smile on my jubilant face. I stressed on the word 'couple' and gave a quick look to Dhruv. "You know, Deb, on this show, I have had stories of self-guilt, discrimination, losing self-worth, and even depression, your story comes as a welcome change," I said.

"I'd say that was unexpected for me too, but my brother stood by me and my family understood. Many aren't as lucky as I am," he stated.

"So, tell me, what are your plans for tomorrow, assuming the ruling decriminalises same sex relations?" I tried to turn the course of discussion to a more pragmatic path.

"I have belief that it will be in our favour, and I'm going to be jubilant about that, maybe I will drink the entire night, or throw a party at my home, or parade in the night waving a rainbow flag; I have no plans yet, but sure I'm going to go out and party hard and raise a toast to rainbow future. It is going to be a never-again tomorrow," he replied, and I could imagine an ecstatic smile across his face, and his eyes gleaming with hope.

Just a reminder to myself: even in the darkest moments, the world held small, quiet corners of hope. One of them bloomed right in my own backyard. When I came out, my family wasn't ready for the truth—I see that now. Understanding takes time. But like me, many will discover that strength often grows close to home, rooted in unexpected places and people. "Great, Anuj, this is going great. Your show has found great support; our social media is brimming with messages in support of the show. We can do a good coverage tomorrow when the ruling comes, and we have already roped in some activists and experts for their comments. We are going to be a full house tomorrow. We are going to come out, loud and proud, as India takes a leap of justice," Dhruv remarked in an exalted, congratulatory tone.

"And we can name our show 'Out, loud and proud,'" Sara at one end added.

"Woah! And that's how a great team works. And when all the brands will get on the race to be the liberal hoppers, we would be hailed as the pioneers. Let's take this as a moment to proudly state to the world that liberalism, justice and compassion are ingredients of a good corporate strategy, and that our channel will always stand for a progressive idea."

I wish I could measure the exuberance in his voice, and as he championed the cause of inclusion, justice and progressive ideas. My heart melted.

***

"It was good today, from one end to the other," I exclaimed as I reached Dhruv's apartment with him.

"It's so nice to see you in this jubilant mode, your eyes gleaming, your forehead sharp and free of any sign of stress, and this joy in your voice," he exclaimed.

I smiled in return, appreciating the deep concern he had shown. "Your house is beautiful," I commented, my voice just above a whisper as I took in all the vibes. I realised that I had not taken it all in due to the pensive mood I had been in the day before.

"Thanks," was all he said as he shut the door behind me. He watched me intently as I looked around like a curious schoolkid.

I noticed a plate of chocolate chip cookies piled on one side and glanced at him. He smiled shyly, and the next moment I was nibbling on them. I heard him give a low laugh as I grabbed a few from the plate and sat on one corner of the couch. I moaned from the deliciousness of the cookies, and he gave his usual, seductive low laugh. I saw his eyes exploring me, diving deep within to find the real me, the jubilant me. I smiled as he smiled, and he came close to me and gave me a passionate kiss.

He wrapped his muscular arm around me and pinioned his legs against mine. My eyes met his deep, dark eyes. A smile set on his face, an enthused smile, a pontifical smile. I moved an inch to accommodate his moves and let him close in on me. His hands sent shivers up my spine as they caressed me. He smirked at me, raising a cute and cocky brow. I felt good as he touched me softly, running his fingers down my neck to my waist, unravelling me as he touched. He slid his hands under my tee and pursed his mouth against mine.

A flurry of passion fashioned me, blood rushed through my veins and heart thundered as I slipped on that path of pleasure and ecstasy. I felt as if my tummy was melting with a mix of nerves and excitement. I moaned as his lips touched the curves and corners of my body and soul. My inner goddess danced with pleasure in an uncontrollable mode, jiving and hopping, as he showered me with kisses. I could be a venetian princess in bed, exulted by every unpredicted move and moulding myself to suit the charm of my prince.

He lowered me slowly and kissed me deeply; his tongue exploring the depths of the vast oceans of passion that resided in me. I brought my hands to caress his back and slowly slid down to explore the volcano of desire in him. I could feel the unmistakable bulge in his pants pressed against my legs. He had an erection, I could feel mine prepared to burst. We halted, took our shirts off and he started nibbling at my body.

I cannot possibly describe the way my body reacted: I was waking up to new and incredible sensations. He had never been this hot before. He had always been the prince who loved slow romance. But this—this was something new. A wilder him had emerged, curious and unrestrained, eager to explore and understand the depths of desire. As he waded against the shallows of my body, he gradually let my body slide, till we were in perfect harmony, something nature would design with its adroit fingers. He was over me and I lay on the couch. He was demanding as he humped and grinded. Yes, that wasn't his usual, he was in his new self that day.

"Should we change our roles today, and you take me?" He whispered in my ears, and all I could do was chuckle at his idea. As he looked at me, I could feel a warm, fuzzy hole burning in my tummy and my whole body trembled uncontrollably with desire.

"We can try that," I moaned as I shifted position and got over him, taking the charge and doing exactly as he did to me, with unmatched passion and vigour.

***

"Wake up, sleepyhead, you are allowed to go to office late, but I need to be there on time. I have some meetings lined up today," Dhruv yelled as he kicked to wake me.

"It was a long night, boy," I groggily said. Ah! He looked so seductive as the morning light slanting from the corners of the curtain shone on one side of his face. How could someone look so fresh and unspoilt after an entire night of lovemaking? I gazed at him like a lovesick bird from the bed.

"I must say you are looking gorgeous." I smiled a sleepy, silly smile.

"You know, I love seeing you like this; waking up half-heartedly, rubbing your eyes in an adorable school-kid way, and saying these lines…that's so heart-stopping beautiful, do you know that?"

"That's a plan to keep you away from work, but then Mr Strategist loves his work more than his boyfriend!" I rolled my eyes as some grumpy kid.

"You know, in Greek mythology, humans had four arms, four legs and two faces. Zeus, fearing their power, split them in two and condemned them to spend their lives searching for their other half. But when I look at you, it feels like Zeus got it wrong—because I didn't have to search at all. You were already mine."

"Oh! Mr flirty strategist, how do you come up with such interesting stories to please me in the morning?" I stood up, all but in my tee, and put my hands around his neck, offering him a solicitous refuge in my loving embrace.

"I believe I will definitely find it in you, if the search can get this beguiling." He smiled and planted a soft kiss on my lips. He took an eyeful of me and whispered, "I have made you breakfast, come to office, when you can," and he rambled towards the hall.

"This 'can' can keep me wondering, you know," I screamed from behind. Sensing he was pretending not to listen and instead making his way to the office, I announced, "I am inviting some friends for dinner today at my place, be there to meet my little hearts…and bye…" He turned in all his confident glory and waved a goodbye kiss.

***

I dressed up fast, it was my day to be on the streets. After the passing of the Privacy bill, it had become obvious that Section 377 was to be read down. Still, my nerves were heightened, a wave of anxiety rushed through me. The 2013 Kaushal vs Naz verdict had come as an end for almost three decades of progress made by the LGBTQIA+ movement in India. Five years, and a ray of hope had become clear. The colonial, archaic section was finally read down. Judge Indu Malhotra got the Apex Court to apologise to the entire LGBTIA+ community for allowing Section 377 to stay on the statute books. The day was to go down as a high watermark, one of modern, post-liberalisation India's most documented struggles.

For millions of us, it was akin to freedom—freedom to be who we were. In 2013, the Apex Court had called the community a 'miniscule minority', but the dogged persistence of this 'miniscule minority' had taken India into the league of liberal nations which respect equality. Though attaining equality and justice in true sense was still a long road, the lovers of liberty had risen to the occasion and fought their way to fashion a way for themselves.

Saying that I was thrilled was an understatement. I was silent, keen on listening, observing and feeling more than expressing.

The happiness was enduring—a quiet, radiant kind. The judgement had done more than affirm our rights; it had given hope, to realise our potential and to express our truths without needing to justify to anyone. The lines were redrawn, they needed to be.

The streets weren't just filled with joy—they pulsed with something deeper—recognition, a collective affirmation of existence. For many, it was the first time stepping into the world as their true selves. Identities long hidden were finally embraced in the open, and countless eyes brimmed with tears —of relief, of pride, of becoming. The whole vibe was inspiring.

I halted to breathe in moments in the heart of Delhi, Connaught Place. The streets looked rainbowed. The streets were alive with a beauty and defiance I had never witnessed before. One judgement couldn't erase decades of taboos, but it had sparked something more powerful: hope.

I knew I'd be celebrating and capturing fragments of joy and resilience. Each face, each story itched itself onto me, leaving an indeliblc imprint on my being. The judgement was a long fight, and just thinking that the day had finally come gave me goosebumps.

As I looked, a young boy, probably in his twenties, came to me with a rainbow flag and smiled. I stretched my hands to take the flag from him, he came close, gave me a half hug and softly whispered 'congrats'.

I managed to hold back my tears. Amazing how a single word could arouse such intense emotions. Or was it just a word? But was it really just a word? No—it carried within it the weight of years. That single word captured years of silent agony within us, of struggling to find ourselves, of enduring the quiet and the loud injustices. That one word held our battles, our resilience, and the hard-won right to finally exist as we are. He held my hand and invited me to the celebrations. There was nothing like obliging. I joined in the merriment, into the music, into the colors, ready to live the countless memories waiting for me that day. I was with my people. I was myself—no, the real me. No masks, no pretence, no living for anyone else. Just me, vibrant and unfiltered, as rainbowed as I've ever been, embracing each moment and every soul I encountered.

Ties That Bind Us

It was certain that there had to be a celebration that night, and because Dhruv had no friends to share it with, he instantly fell in with my plans. I was tired —messages flooding in, calls to answer, interviews to give, and countless stories shared through the show. It had been a whirlwind of a day. Romantic songs filled the air, and our people were out on the streets capturing the narratives, as hundreds and thousands came out. Many ghosts were laid to rest that day.

I waited for him eagerly as I prepared drinks for everyone. I wanted him to meet everyone I held close—my little pieces of heart.

"It's your day, Anu. Stop dwelling on your past. And focus on the future—on where and how you want to take this further." My sister scowled when I told her about my break-up with Nikhil. I nodded but shrugged at the same time. Why did I even bring that up? Probably deep down, I still held him in high regard. Probably.

"Not to butt in the sibling talk here, but when is the light of the party coming? Have heard so many confessions, I can't wait to meet him now." Dhriti cocked her eyebrows.

"You make yourself a drink, he will come when he has to," I muttered.

"See, that's why you should never date those senior managers, they go bum at these times," Aarya added in a mocking tone, trying to make his presence felt in the party.

After years of dilly-dallying and the shared insolence of preferring live-in to marriage, Aarya and Dhriti had finally agreed to tie the knot last year. Nikhil had found an excuse to not be there, and his absence had pierced me. It was then that the cracks in our relationship became painfully clear. That was our story, and it had run its course. But if I had not met Dhruv, and by God's handiwork, we had not fallen for each other, would I have been capable of being in a celebratory mode as I was in that moment? I shuddered to think that. I shuddered at the thought of not having the present I had.

And perhaps for an iota of a moment, I wanted to blame myself for not preparing for the collapse of my deftly knitted relationship, when all the cues of it failing were around me. Why did I choose to hang on than just run away and shape a future I wanted? Why do we all love hanging on or holding onto broken and shattered things? Is accepting the end of things and running away from them so difficult, or do we just keep affirming the decisions made in the past?

And then, there he was—Dhruv, his face lit with a beatific smile. I rushed to him. And for a brief moment, everything froze. The hum of the party didn't matter and the people around became non-existent. An unknown feeling empowered me like air laden with a sense of snow and gone wild with its playful thoughts. It was the feeling of awakening — like the fire's warm breath tickling the log, unaware of the glow it sparked; like soft music threading its way through the rustle of leaves. In that instant, it felt like lives collapsed between two smiles; and all that existed was a quiet, profound poetry — one kindled by hope and compassion.

"And look, there you are! We've all been waiting for you to officially celebrate this new chapter in our lives," my sister, a little tipsy by then, announced in her typical overzealous voice.

"She's my older sister, and she's the one who outed me to our parents. It's a long story, one I'll have to tell you sometime" I said holding onto his arms.

"Hey, I was a bitch then; and it took me time to understand everything. And it was just unintentional. But I still feel sorry about that."

"It happens. We can't complain about that. All that matters is that today, you stand by his side," he replied, such a caring, pacifying tone.

"Congratulations to you both. Such a way to celebrate Anuj. Gosh! I must say I am happy for you" Niharika, my friend, gave a salubrious smile as she shook hands with Dhruv.

"This is Niharika. And this darling has recently moved in with her girlfriend, defying every ordeal," I said chirpily, giving a soft punch on her shoulders.

"I am so happy to see you both together," Niharika said.

"And I could say the same for you. I am happy this angel came in my life..." Dhruv replied, smiling as he half-hugged me in appreciation.

"And here we have this beautiful couple, Aarya and Dhriti, my college friends, my besties who tied the nuptial knot last year. This guy is a total charmer, and he also happened to be my roommate in college. Dhriti, on the other hand, is the rational babe; we survived graduation thanks to her notes and after lecture classes…old-timers basically," and I could not help laughing as a wave of memories of those days washed over me.

"Well, what he forgot to tell you is that I am his agony aunt, and if you ever want to know anything about him, all you need is to text me," she jibed.

"I can say that discovering things on our own has a different ring to it. And if he ever gets pissed with me, which I would never want to happen, I shall reach out to you to find easy ways to get this devil to set things down."

Dhruv was a quintessential charmer: soft-spoken, ever ready with a smile, effortlessly eloquent, and always slaying with his timeless style and elegant combinations. It didn't take him much time to win many hearts at the party.

***

I don't know how it started—or even why. It wasn't the kind of occasion meant for heavy conversations. But I suppose we were all in a different mood that day: joyful, overwhelmed, maybe just craving a release, or maybe it was just those two rounds of Vodka that stirred this. It was Rehan, a dear friend of mine, who began it. He tried to sum up the day, and in doing so, found himself drifting into the story of how he came out.

"Acceptance is something that pushes you over—an act of anxiety or desperation. It was confusing to me, and I wasn't prepared to accept that. I found myself sinking when I first got physically intimate with someone of my own sex. Until then, it was all locked somewhere inside me. And it never seemed unusual. But that touch—it stirred me—first I felt wrong, then I got anxious, I resisted, and then I longed. It took me time to accept what was happening. All my life I was subjected to such heteronormative narratives, and those rights and wrongs, that my own desires and feelings appeared alien to me. I was confused; I panicked."

"There was chaos in my mind. It took me time to tell myself that there was no wrong in it, and that I needed it, and I had been yearning for it." Rehan was the first one to go as we sat to share our midnight 'being gay' stories.

"And when did this happened to you? In your school?" My sister asked out of curiosity. I don't remember but maybe it was she who encouraged this conversation.

Rehan answered with a nod of his head. "Yes, it happened there. School can be a merciless place. We were young, and supportive and bully to each other, all at the same time. But that incident taught me about myself, and about what I wanted. But I felt weak, and I don't know for how long I kept questioning myself. I think it was only when I shifted to Delhi that I felt a little free," Rehan added.

"You know, mine is a funny story. Well, there may be a better word to describe it, but I see it as funny. Like an unwanted kind of funny. My mother came to know of my sexuality when she was going through my books, and she found a note I had written to another girl. Gosh! Just imagine the horror of your mother finding out the truth through a note. And this just doesn't end there. In that same note I had written awful things about my parents. When she questioned me, I could only scream in shock. I am just glad she kept this to herself. It took her almost two years to come to terms with my truth. It still comes up in conversations, at times. She still wishes I were like other girls. I just feel eventually, there will be peace between us." Niharika told her story, almost gloomy, her voice low and torn.

Coming out is often framed as that one major, almost imperative event in every queer person's life: a moment from which a person can start 'being themselves'.

"It was I who outed Anuj," announced my sister. "And it just happened, I acted like that ass of a sister who read her brother's chats, and that one asinine moment made me realise how much my brother hid from me. I was, honestly sad, that Anuj was unable and unwilling to share these things. I wanted to be that support and understand more, but I was stupid. I probably kept overstepping. It was difficult for me to comprehend everything," my sister related.

"But you did—and you've been a pillar ever since. I couldn't have done it without you. God hasn't exactly gifted me a light heart. I honestly don't know how I would have made it through without you, Dhriti and Aarya. It was like, I was holding a lot within me. With you people around, I could open up, even in fragments, and ease the weight" I said, a hand squeezing my heart, reflecting on the tumultuous journey I went through while opening up, first to my sister, then my friends and finally my parents. That last part... that was the hardest of all.

I looked at Dhruv, he was quiet, he had been quiet all along. I didn't know his side of the story, but by now I had at least come to know that there was possibly some fear lurking inside him. Or was I just brooding too much? I reached across and brushed my hand against his. His expression softened and relaxed.

***

That was my small support group: a couple of friends I had made, a sister who meant more than parents, and a handful of like-minded people I met as I discovered myself.

For Dhruv, possibly, I was the only one. I realised how difficult it could get if there were none to share your thoughts with. It's always a cauldron of emotions inside our hearts. I knew so little of his past, yet I could sense the weight of it—the hidden stories tucked away in shadow, the ones that shaped his quiet mystery and made him feel at once elusive and almost otherworldly.

I looked at him again, in the hope of filtering through his eyes and knowing more about him. He looked at me passively, not moving, not saying anything. We didn't talk much, and I could sense his reluctance. I stayed on, waiting for the party to disperse. He was staying back with me, and I wanted to feel the fear that hung in his sordid eyes.

"What happened to you? You look sad and anxious," I asked, my voice a whisper emanating from the depths of my psyche.

"I honestly don't know what to say. I never felt this heavy and burdened before. As you people talked, there were so many thoughts whirring in my mind," he answered, voice as low as mine.

"You know I kinda hated it. I didn't want things to go this gloomy. It was my sister, now I am certain of it. I don't know why she feels so guilt-ridden. But you know if there's something you wish to talk about, I am always there to listen to," I said on a shuddering breath, as I read reluctance drawn long on his face.

He came close and kissed me long and hard. "Why do you press?" He asked.

"Because I can see you are holding something inside you, and that it's eating you from inside," I murmured. I held his hands.

"Fair enough, I will share everything with you someday, I assure you, I will. But for today, let's just sleep and not make this long night become longer," he said.

That Cold Evening

I could hear the bells from a religious procession nearby. I followed the procession, gaining an uncertain calmness in the bells. I had abandoned myself to the sound, which wound around my waist like a rope, binding me in its hypnotic wrap. Above me stretched the labyrinth of the starry sky; beneath my feet, its reflection shone in relief — the earthy ground, blades of grass, thick undergrowth, lined by tall trees on the sides.

The wind carried the chill of the coming winters. I had come out for a walk, leaving Dhruv, who had chosen to remain indoors and work. I wanted to give him space to work. Above the moon shone—immense, still, pensive. The night was unusually calm, and I loved that calmness; something in me desired that. The stillness of the night seemed so calming after days of hustle.

I took a detour to a nearby park, finally uncoiling myself from that sound. I sat there in silence, an uninvited guest in that wilderness. Boom and echo rose above the silence of the place. I called my sister and told her everything. I told her of Dhruv's child abuse and whatever he had said to me. I was content, prepared to deal with the situation. I didn't need her approval or validation, only that she knew that I didn't want to hide it from her.

"Are you worried?" She asked. Was I? Perhaps more befuddled than worried. And more befuddled because Dhruv was worried. Dhruv was a silent mess, and I knew so little of him. He kept his worries locked in himself and opened that lock occasionally to sink into his past. And then there were moments when he appeared so distant, all when so seemingly close to me. It was all a mirage—a sad feeling disguised as some celestial form, gliding with radiance, arms outstretched, beckoning me to follow it.

I smiled in bewilderment. I wanted to know everything he hid in him, I wanted to know the child in him who was abused, a growing teen who lived in a nightmarish reality, a lover who buried his love, a prodigal son who lived a love-hate relation with his mother, and a boy who had broken most of the family ties. He was an enigma, or just a silent mess. But whatever he was, I wished to know him.

"You can only really relive what you've already been through. But even then, nothing ever comes back exactly the same. So just keep going. The understanding will come, eventually. Be there for him, if you want to know him. He'll open up someday. Maybe he wants to already… he just doesn't know how," she said.

I knew she was hinting at me and my habit of holding everything to myself, and how she had to always prod me to know. I would open only when I had prepared my mind; her prodding never worked. And Dhruv would do the same, open when he wished to; no prodding would work.

***

I ensured my composure was restful to him and acted as ballast to his somewhat unstable sensibilities. He was stepping out and trusting me to reveal some dark unknowns of his life. We had been appreciative of each other so far, and that was the time to build our relationship into something more meaningful. As for him who survived the darkness, I needed those disclosures to understand who he really was. I knew I was the unwanted pest who survived on truths, that had ruined things with Nikhil before, but the quest for truth was undeniably and inconvincibly ingrained in me.

A part of Dhruv only existed in the private darkness, for it was there that the doubts, fears, anxieties, and tribulations of the man the world knew as Dhruv disappeared. They were shed totally, but only for the time when the room remained in darkness. And in that darkness, a young child who had seen and felt more than he should have, emerged. For me, it was important to know that child, to know Dhruv.

I lay down beside him, rested one hand on his chest, the other pillowed, to hear him intently.

"Why are you so intent on listening to the story? It's just a bad memory I don't want to talk about. Let it remain locked. It will only hurt if it comes out," he said, tears filling his eyes.

"And that's why I want you to talk about it and free yourself of that shame or guilt or fear or anything it is. Don't hide it. You know you have failed in that attempt," I consoled. I didn't know if I was overstepping or trying to build the trust that could take our relationship far. But whatever it was, I was going far too strongly, and I was making him do the unwanted.

"I had a traumatic childhood, Anu. Bad things happened, and I have never been able to share them with anyone —never, not even with my mother. I request you not to press me to disclose that. It hurts. And I don't want a dark memory to tarnish the beauty of what we have. We have a future to think about. Let the past remain buried. I've shared what it was and how hard it was for me; going into details will only cause more pain." A stream of tears rolled down his cheeks. For a moment, the person who, to me, embodied every fairy tale prince seemed an irreparable loss.

"You can trust me, but tell me when you are ready. I won't coax you to share it." I said. I knew he'd open up when he wanted, and even if he chose not to, it was his prerogative. I had decided to walk that path with him —to embrace his darkness, live through the shadows that chased him, and face the confusion that faced him.

I switched off the lights. I didn't want to ask anything more, and he wanted his space. I positioned my legs to his and spooned around him to sleep. I could feel the warmth of his breath. His breathing was slow, like that of a perturbed soul, or one who wanted to slow down to escape his past. I could feel his desire for togetherness. I knew his need arose from his fears. The conversation that night had opened a wound in him. His terrified soul had been touched.

***

It was a cold evening, like many others before. The cold breeze shrieked and carried a strange feeling with it. There had been no sign or promise of sun the entire day. There seemed to be an indescribable darkness over the face of things. Something seemed to have died, or forgotten, or lost forever. The pain was more than the indescribable uncertainty that hung in my life. It carried the malaise of ages, and the cold wind was heavy with the burden of those unspoken cries.

For miles, there was nothing —just the ancient forest, standing still, witness to the many stories long forgotten. The trees rose like an apparition, solemn and watchful. The world had shifted —or perhaps it had grown too cold, entangled in the web of its own complications.

My mother sat outside on the lawn that opened to the forest. On the other side were the tea estates that we owned. She breathed in the cold mess of the place —the age-old rivalries, and the deep-seated parochialism that once drove her away in search of a life she believed she could build for herself. Alas! She didn't know what she left behind would one day ensnare her son, a wound left open, a scar that never healed. She took a deep breath, trying to take in a lion's share of oxygen, albeit it could come to haunt her sometime. As it is said, sometimes the things that look the safest hide the gravest of dangers.

Dephny crouched down on her haunches and waited until my mother could see her through the blur of her tears.

"I am sorry for the loss of your mother. I can imagine your pain," she said.

"It is fine; you don't have to feel bad. She was old, and we knew this would come sooner or later. We thought we were mentally prepared for it, but it happened suddenly, far sooner than we had expected. I never expected to be left so alone, so quickly and so abruptly."

Dephny handed my mother a tissue. My mother sniffed as she said, "You're very good. I am grateful to you that you took care of my mother till her last breath, and that you have been good to my son. I have been a bit lost in everything around me to take care of my duties," she replied, taking the tissue from her and wiping tears that had rolled down her eyes for her mother, whom she just occasionally saw.

"Calm down. Let me make you tea or coffee?"

"Tea, please. No milk, and two sugar cubes."

Dephny made a charade out of brewing the tea to allow the silence to settle. An elegant twirl of copper fell from the teapot into their China cups. The soft clink of spoons echoed as they stirred in their sugar cubes.

She held a thought in her mind before speaking again, less to strike up a conversation and more to break the haunting silence. She hated it, she hated this silence, and that had made her leave this damn place. "Since when have you been here, Dephny?"

"Five or six years easily, started as managing the administration of an estate, and then your mother asked me to come home and take care of things here."

"Ah, so you were here when we brought Dhruv, I didn't know that," my mother remarked as she took a sip of her tea. Dephny nodded in agreement.

My mother had a tumultuous life. Hardly had she known that trouble ran in our genes. She decided to leave the place when the silence of the hills became haunting for her. She wanted to drift with the waves of the Arabian Sea. Her calling was from Mumbai, a life she had dreamt of. She fled from another life to chase her dreams, leaving behind everything that once defined her. She came back only to leave me to the mercy of the whining winds that plunged the valley into inescapable silence. She told me my nana (grandmother) would take care of me, as she busied herself sorting her life and working on her dreams. But in our sad lives, even dreams came with a price, sometimes a price too heavy to pay.

A lonely child like me only grew lonelier in that huge estate, where there were many people to take care of me, but none I could grow with. Nana was old, and her compassion had boundaries. And with every passing day, she became more indifferent to everything around her, even her grandson. I existed for her, but hardly mattered to her.

"Trust me, ma'am, he is good here. You need not worry about him. I know you have many things to take care of in Mumbai, he'll do well here."

"I love you for this, Dephny, I really do. But I think my boy needs his mother now. And I don't think I have been a good mother in the past three years. Dealing with all the shit in my life, I had forgotten I have a kid to take care of. I cannot thank you enough for taking care of my growing kid, but it's time for a mother to build a life with her son." She stated her will, more pronounced by the tears in my eyes than her concern. My mother always knew when to take over the entire conversation and push her views on others. And she had often proven right while thrusting her views.

She stood up and strolled to the end that overlooked the forest. She crossed her hands as she walked. She wasn't used to the cold. Under her jacket was a letter wrapped in her handkerchief. The letter I had kept beside her bed that morning as she lay asleep. She had started to love the same silence that she had left many years back. It allowed her to reflect, dream of a life she could have given herself. With her grit, she had built a life truer than any man's judgment could ever grasp.

She opened the letter to read it. I couldn't have faced her. I had called her three days back and could say no word. I wanted to write down everything, but the thought of telling everything had stopped me. What I wrote was just a scratch of what I had in my mind. A string of tears rolled down her cheeks as she read the letter. She clasped her face with both her hands. She looked at the insurmountable amount of loss around her. Her mother had died, her life was anything but a mess, and her son lived a troubled life. She rubbed her hands to provide warmth. No matter how much she rubbed, the instant she stopped, her face and nose would become numb. She knew the numbness arose more from the eerie situation she was in than the cold wind. There were no easy solutions. There had never been.

"Ma'am, it will be better to step in and sit beside the fire. It's cold outside, and you are not quite used to it." She could hear Dephny's voice beating the shrill of the wind.

She turned, looked at the huge bungalow that wore a macabre look, and nodded to Dephny's call. She moved suddenly like a frightened horse, losing herself to the haunting thoughts as she strode towards the bungalow.

Mom came to see me in my room. I sat on a couch, hiding a deep secret. She came and sat next to me, taken aback by the frigid me. "You wrote in a letter that you fear something; over the call that day, you kept on crying. Won't you tell me what scares you so badly?" She asked her fourteen-year-old son in a voice as low as possible.

I wasn't used to this affection from her. I was too drowned in my fears, clouded by uncertainty, and in a deep ocean full of despair, gasping for some breath. Why didn't I ever reach out to her? She was my mother after all. Had I, she would have listened and eased my pain. Perhaps I would, had she shown that sort of concern before. Or was it just the situations that had left her stranded and scared, too? Could I have spoken to her when she was herself broken and deserted? Or was the young boy sitting on a couch, with dried eyes and scarred soul, ever capable of that argument? I was hurt too, buried in my sorrows, those thoughts wouldn't have come to me. The two broken souls could have been each other's saviour, had one spoken to the other, tried to enquire about the other, or just apprised of one's sorrow. They could have held each other.

"Say something to your mother," she said again, clasping my face in her hands, her eyes deep, wet, and fixed.

"Take me from here," I could only manage. I embraced her to pour out the ocean of despair caged in my heart. She hugged me tightly. All questions, all answers washed away in those tears. She said nothing, and I spoke nothing. We both sobbed till our hearts melted and our eyes dried. And in that moment, a hurting mother and a hurting son came close, closer than they had ever been before. But not close enough to lay bare their hearts and let the demons out. Their fears remained in their closets, locked and well-preserved.

"I will. And I'm very sorry you had to live without me. I don't even have the right words with me, but please... forgive me," she said with a deep strain of anguish in her voice. She felt the pain of her son's troubled mind. She knew that while she remained busy trying to put her life in order, she couldn't fathom the turmoil in her son's life.

***

I woke up in the dead of the night, not finding Dhruv sleeping beside me. He was standing on the balcony, brooding. His eyes blinked at the sky, oblivious to the thousands of questions clouding his senses. Beneath, a shadow lurked, tormenting and vandalising his soul. A sharp line of anxiety was drawn on his usually genial face. I stepped out to talk to him. September night is usually not the best time to step out and brace oneself to the changing weather.

"You aren't sleeping?" I asked groggily, putting my hand on his shoulder.

"I am not finding sleep," he replied, words seemed to get stuck out of immeasurable pain.

I leaned on the balcony wall to face him. "Hey, look at me…" He cocked his head to look at me, his face flaccid. "You don't have to tell me, and you don't have to get worried. Whatever it was, it's now the past. You are out of that," I said, feeling unconvinced of my own words. I regretted my doltish act, trying to open the sealed wound just because I thought I could heal it if I knew. It was deeper than I had thought, like a string of fear that had remained with him, an old curse or an unforgiving old tale. I held his hand and took him in. I pulled the drapes again to darken the room. He rested his head on my chest. I clasped his face with one hand and ran the other through his hair.

He would usually sleep for hours. If I let him, he would sleep the whole day. He loved to sleep in a way I didn't, sliding into it at every chance; it was like his native element, whereas almost always, I slept poorly, uneasily, and waking up early. It was the opposite that day. I could only hate myself for bringing up that topic, but then it was as apropos as the thought of trust between us.

I was usually the one to get up soon. Mornings were time to spend on my writing and myself; I would get up soon and spend time looking at his sleep-smoothened face, often sit beside him, cup his face in my palms, and run my fingers through his messy, still smooth hair. He would usually duck to avoid being him in his sleep. He would urge him to allow him to sleep more, and I would laugh, my high-pitched morning laugh, more of a shrill chuckle. Even this annoyance was a part of our love. We were so early and in love.

But it was different that day, very different from the usual. His sleep was rugged, disturbed by the unkind memories of the past and the horrors he had buried. I had opened his wounds with my questions, showing no mercy in my insistence to know them.

I woke up and looked at my boy. He slept with his hands straddling under his head. I caught my breath at it. I felt a weird pressure and heat climb my throat. I felt my heart ache, that was the phrase for it, a sullen, unforgiving feeling, drifting in me like an electric pulse. I wished to hug him, lest it disturb him in his sleep. And I wished a lot—to laugh with him till our stomachs ache, to smile with him until my cheeks hurt, to kiss him until the lips become numb, to be in love with him, madly, utterly in love with him, to build on the promises and hold his secrets, and to be with him in the best and worst times of his life. That morning, I wanted him to be how I had always seen him.

I Won't Let the Darkness Cast a Shadow on You

I prepared breakfast when he woke. I prepared his favourite *chole-puri*. He was fond of it, and all I wanted was for him to feel at ease, to find some comfort. I took an eyeful of him as I took a sip of my morning coffee. He had slept a disturbed sleep. By then, I had lost interest to know his childhood; it evoked an emotion of fear in me, a fear of losing him to despair. There was a certain corporate airlessness to our lives, each of us grappling with their fears in silence, unable to open up, paralyzed by the weight of unspoken words. These are unseen boundaries of the toxic masculine environment we've all been raised in, shaping our identities, while erasing our individualities.

It was around nine in the morning. The sky pushed on and on. Great swathes of blue. The sun shone brightly, another hot day.

"Why didn't you wake me up? I'll be late for office," he said in a woozy tone.

"I didn't want to disturb you. Last night was a sort of everything, late-night party and then a disturbing conversation. And you were unable to catch good sleep in the night, so I thought an extra hour is something you can afford. I thought it would be fine to let you sleep an extra hour."

"Stop blaming yourself. I guess it's fine. Nothing will change if I reach the office an hour or two late."

"I have made your favourite *chole-puri,* so better get freshened up fast for I want to have breakfast together. And after breakfast, I need your well whipped nowhere else on earth coffee."

"Why are you such a dole of love?" He said, giving a flirtatious smile. I couldn't resist smiling, not at how flirtatious he could get but how relieving seeing him smile was for me.

"You know, I was wondering last night if we can go somewhere together, like travel together to a romantic place, check in a cosy resort, and lead a laidback life with good amount of sunshine, and perfect beaches. Some place like Bali or Maldives?" I muttered. The thought had been floating in my mind for days.

"Well, I am more of a history buff than a beach person but I won't mind a place that can offer both. And I'm always in for long, lovely walks and doles of good food," he replied, putting on his shirt.

I did want to travel with him, to a place where there was no pressure of secrecy, where you could hold hands in the streets, kiss in public, however chastely, where nowhere we had to keep a casual distance lest someone notice and give us a long stare, and a place where there was none to judge us for how close we walked to each other; I wanted to be with him in a place where we could be freer with each other. I could gift him that, a getaway, a bit of romance.

"That sounds something like Europe to me—Italy precisely." I chuckled, mastering my own game.

"You know me so well," he replied with a cheeky grin, knowing well that I had aimed my shot precisely, and there was no way he could deflect the volley of shots from there.

"I will take the planning into my hands." I said, sounding like a giddy child.

"My pleasure. But there is a lot to be sorted out here as I am gradually taking command of the family business. So, babes, just tarry a little. And don't worry, I would love to travel the entire world with you."

"What family business, you never told me," I asked inquisitively, clearing a space on the table for breakfast, shifting the plates around until one almost tipped onto the floor; he caught it just in time.

"Babes, my mother holds stakes in the place you work in… and my mother owns the Mad House advertising firm," he replied in as modest a tone he could manage.

"Fuck! Mad House advertising…your mother…oh fuck, does that mean…*The* Melissa Shankar is your mother…I mean *The Melissa Shankar!*" I cried, both surprised and amused. "Fuck, she is the goddess of the advertising business. Fucking Dhriti would die to work with her…holy fuck, I am dating my employer, not my boss but my employer!" I don't think I would have ever used so many fucks in one sentence, and there he was putting *chole* in the bowls. He looked up at me and shrugged, and I stood there in disbelief. That was a little too much of information and imagination in one go to fathom. Melissa Shankar, someone we had read about and aspired to be; I was fucking dating her son… Holy heavens!!

"Well, I was afraid to tell you this, not knowing how you would react to it. And then, I never thought it was important to bring this between us, and eventually you were to know, so a little wait wouldn't have done any damage. Maybe I should have told you the truth."

"Whatever! All plans cancelled, now let's go to Bora Bora islands. I am dating a fucking business tycoon!" I teased, still trying to breathe in the truth I was made aware of during a normal, breakfast-time conversation.

He served me another puri. "Well, if Dhriti wants to get mad in a Mad House and work with the goddess of the advertising business— 'The Melissa Shankar'—I can put in a word for her," he said, almost imitating me, with a strong emphasis on 'the Melissa Shankar'. He could say so, but for people like us, she was a name to reckon with. I looked at him and could easily see through the expression he was wearing. There was genuine warmth in his eyes, but even that warmth was unable to settle my nerves.

"I'll tell her I have taken the boy, she can take the mother," I answered in a delectably spiced up tone.

"Oh, please don't do that, I don't want unnecessary gossip to erupt. I can't take all that attention," he replied teasingly. My eyes lit with amusement. "And we should meet my mom, whenever you feel ready. We can go to Mumbai anytime."

"Oh, I would love to do that. Who won't, she is quite an inspiration. You know we read about the phenomenal ads she made." I said, rolling my eyes, and he smiled looking at the feisty me.

"Well, you can meet mom and tell her how phenomenal she is."

"Haha, anytime —let's make it today!" He rolled his eyes, more like saying 'LOL' with them.

"By the way when I said we can meet her, I was also hinting at we meeting her as partners, which is you meeting her as the love of her son's life. Because I really want to come out to my mother, and I need you by my side when I do that." Touched, I reached out to squeeze his hand. That statement meant something.

"Are you sure?" I said. My voice sounded low but hard. He nodded his head and gazed evenly at me. I smiled, for that was the only thing I could do. Inside, my heart squeezed. These are rare moments in anyone's life, and I was having mine.

"We can go together to office; I hope you won't mind that," he asked.

"I am sorry to butt things down here. It's okay to take things slow, especially in a workplace. It's a different and unpredictable setup, why invite stares and questions. People know about me; it won't be hard for them to figure things out and start corridor whispers. Better we avoid that; at least for some time." I looked across the table at Dhruv, who was gazing at me openly, hopefully, boyishly.

"Got it," he said plaintively. "I think I am just overwhelmed getting this ravishing, beauty in my life, and like some school kid I want to go all out and scream out to the world that this guy is my boy," he said, almost hopefully.

I clung to him like I was clinging to a cliff, and he clung right back. "Hold your horses," I whispered in his ear.

***

"Look at you! Where were you, such a mess you have become," Dephny cried, looking at me as I stood in an unrecognisable form. Cold perspiration beading up on a flushed face. She looked at me; I felt ashamed. It had happened again.

"Who did this to you?" She asked. "Did you pick up a fight again?"

"Yes," I responded, looking rather confused. I again hid the truth from her. She hugged me. I could sense she somehow knew the truth. "It won't happen again," I mumbled as I swung myself around on the stool and faced in the other direction. I said this to myself every time it happened. I knew those smiling piranhas had planned on chewing me up and spitting out the bones, and I had to stand and fight for myself. But it happened again, and I hid it every time it happened. I pictured myself as the one standing aggressively against those bullies, hands on hips, watching their fast-disappearing forms as they beat a hasty retreat into the swirling fog. But I could never face my bullies.

"You will need medicines, go clean yourself and then I will dress your wounds," she said in her usual salacious tone. "Your school fights are becoming a regular affair. I understand this happens in your age, but let it not go to your grandma and then your mother. Things are not good at their end, and we should avoid giving them unnecessary trouble. Hope you understand. And for yourself, you need to sort this thing out, or if you wish, I can come with you and discuss with your teachers," she said in a part concerned, and part scathing tone.

I did understand, and I wish I shouldn't have. Hardly had I known that another ordeal was to start that day, one that I was completely unprepared for, both physically and mentally.

Dephny waited with a first-aid box for me. I cleansed the wounds with water to remove the dirt and came out. She asked me to take off my shirt. I did as was instructed. "Is it a fight or you're getting beaten and not telling me?" She asked, applying Dettol on my wounds. I stood starkly silent. "Did you throw your butts at someone, like some cheesy, weary girl?" I sweated in the still cold air, as she hurled taunts at me. "Feels you want your pretty face all smashed up." A cloud of halitosis-tainted steam was ejected towards me.

This was the fourth time in the span of a fortnight. Dephny certainly knew what I was going through in school. She kept that a secret. Prior intimidation at school had ensured my silence. I looked at her as she applied ointment on my wounds, tears rolling down my eyes.

"You have to man yourself up boy, the world is hard," she said and stared at me in amusement. She chuckled, looked into my eyes, holding my gaze, and with one hand she wiped my tears and the other she rolled on my naked chest. "Let's teach you some tricks and spank this shit off you." She clasped my face with her hands and stared into my eyes, a wicked grin spread on her assumingly salubrious face.

I looked at her with trepidation, unaware, almost petrified at the sudden change in her behaviour. She inched closer and forced her mouth onto mine, snuggling me tight, her one hand clasped against my head and the other exploring the curves of my shoulders and back.

When her lips parted, I saw it in her eyes—the red haze of lust, but not for desire; it was lust for domination. I felt my grip on reality slipping further and further away, like I was being pulled into something I couldn't escape. I was a coward, so scared I couldn't run, even if I wanted to, even if there had been anywhere to go. Deep down, the-little-boy-who-was-still-me quaked in abject fear. I silently choked back sobs, my throat tight with unshed tears. The panic controlled me; I stood there dumb, unaware, letting her have what she wanted.

She ran her hands all over my face, her words laced with mockery. "I'll make a man out of you," she snorted mildly. And the next moment, she pushed me onto the bed. I tried to scream, but she pressed a finger on my mouth and signalled me to remain quiet, as she explored my body. A low sound escaped me, a mix of fear and helplessness—too terrified to say something, too afraid to even scream and call for my grandma. She did what she wanted, and my cowardice let her do that. Her dark eyes sank into my soul, ravaging it, shredding the innocence in it, piercing the most sacred corners like a lurking monster.

Her unimaginably warm hands dug into my head as she forced herself on me. "What, don't be afraid, there is nothing wrong in this," she murmured and started kissing my neck, running the tip of her tongue down my throat. She towered over me, gazing down. And then she went further down and buried herself in my nether region; she kissed, bit and sucked me, all the while I cried, a cry too low for someone to listen.

After she was gone, I hid my face between my knees and wept for more than an hour. I felt broken and completely shaken by what was done to me. I recollected my senses and tried to gather what was left of me. That instant, I had transpired into a different person, one precipitating in a state of psychological chaos and pain. I looked in the mirror, trying to count the number of marks on my body, unable to differentiate who had caused what. I held a hard, obtuse look on my face. My body ached. My hands trembled.

Could I have been able to recount what had happened, if they had asked? I was not certain, but then there was no one to ask. My grandmother had given up on my frequent fights, never wondering about the real reason behind them, or how an introvert kid like me could pick fights. She never noticed that I had no friends to invite over at our bungalow, or that I always preferred staying at home than going out to play. Probably Dephny had noticed my vulnerabilities and taken upon herself to make a man out of me, as she put it.

I looked out of the window. It was seven o'clock and the sun's long journey had ended. The evening felt pleasant. The soft breeze blew gently over my face. I had spent four hours locked up in my room, sobbing, in a pensive, thoughtless state. And there was no one to care. My mother would call me every three-four day, and my grandma was indifferent and too sick to make up for the huge emotional void that defined my life. Dephny cared for me—nursed my wounds, listened to my stories, and filled the emotional void in my life—but her compassion came at a price. My thoughts flickered like a candle flame, dancing in the over-warmed breeze. I felt drained.

I skipped my dinner that night. And such a fool of me to think I could escape my destiny by killing my appetite. Late in the night, Dephny came to my room with the dinner. "If you will not eat, how will you grow and stand up to those bullies?" Grasping my chin, she forced my eyes to meet hers. Her looks were intimidating. "Now eat," she said, her voice almost devoid of all emotion.

I ate. And as I ate, her eyes explored me, her piercing gaze remained fixed on me. "I have told your grandmother that I will be sleeping with you tonight. She was quite relaxed to hear that. She knows I care for you and that I love you," she said unapologetically.

"No, I am fine," I mustered some strength to say that.

"And we know you aren't. So why don't you do as I say? Because I am the only one who can hear you in this big house..." Her words ruptured me. I felt helpless.

I looked out of the window. The moon shone brightly in the clear skies; its beauty was blazing. Its silver splendour ran through the dark alleys of my being; chasing me, hurting me with its pristine beauty. I wished I could drown in its splendour and wake up as another being in some other place.

***

"You know, let's do the Amy Hempel, and you tell me something foolish that I won't mind forgetting," I said. "Make it useless stuff. Enough of serious talks. You talk such serious shit every time, and it starts hitting the mind after a while."

Dhruv looked at me and rolled his eyes. We were walking to the nearby café to have tea and some munchies. We desperately needed a break, both from the two-hour long discussion that random newspaper headlines pushed us into, and my compulsive evening healthy snacks. By now, I had got into the habit of marking my cheat moments from vegan life—two times a week was allowed.

And he started. He made up stories as he talked. And by the time we reached the café, I had listened to uncanny stories of how the world would change if insects learned to sing, and birds to swim. And by the then standards of our uselessness, all that was palatable. We congratulated ourselves to live and make the other person live fantasy, for reality had become too tiring for us. We usually talked serious stuff and found ourselves repeating the same thing in a loop albeit in different words. And so, after a time, there remained hardly a thing to add.

The worst would come when we got into scientific folds and two people who had never studied physics debated like some physicists of the 'no-bother' land on scientific theories. And to shy all the creepiness in life and be more scientific in our arguments, we would read scientific papers and discuss, at times for hours. And we did this often when we got bored of our usual talks. Sports and culture did come up occasionally, but those were his domains, and I'd be left dumbstruck. So, my inflated ego usually steered us away from them, gravitating instead toward topics where we either both had something or absolutely nothing—to say. Strangely, the ones where we were both clueless turned out to be the most fun, because then we had a third companion: Lord Google.

"What else? Have you got something gossipy to tell?" For me, he would always have something else.

"Oh, yes, do you know when scientists first taught chimpanzees to talk, they lied," he said in his usual 'you know I'm kidding' look.

"That's a good one, a nice parable. We should add this as one of the scientific reasons to say that we evolved from them?" I joked. He looked at me and burst into laughter.

And we laughed and talked a little more, feeling like some outlaws, before we reached the café.

"Should we order some nachos and tea?"

"You know the rules, one with the best story gets to order. The chimpanzee one was good humour, I'll give you today's chance for that," I said giddily. "You know, I wish to keep a cat," I said merrily.

"Why not a dog? Cats have tantrums, and then I will have to manage tantrums of two beings," he bantered and gave a half-smile.

"No, dogs are judgmental. They say the smart dog obeys, but the smarter dog knows when to disobey."

"Yes," he said, "the smarter anything knows when to disobey."

"Now you are trying to smart-mouth me. But if it is only my desire to keep an animal then we can go with a cat, an easy to manage creature, fluffy, with limited expressions and demands," I sniped.

"Cats are quite demanding creatures, if you are willing to take the load. Let's do this when we shift together."

"So, cat it is, maybe that way you will learn how to respond to tantrums," I said, stuck in my irrational state of mind. And I continued, "But you know, I have started to love this therapy of concocting stories and taking a break from the sensible stuff we read and utter all day. It keeps my creative juices running high," I added.

"Hold on a minute. Tell me, is it your company, or this tea, or the after-effect of all the irrational stuff we have been talking about, that I got this wonderful idea?" he said with a faintly sneering smile, as though we were both in on the joke. I inclined in anticipation of another cock and a bull story. "We can do a satirical radio show on these serious shits like politics, sports or even current affairs. Not the usual stuff, but something tackier than practiced. Something deeper, more informed, but presented in a more palatable fashion."

I leaned back in my chair and smacked my head with my hands, trying to appear thoughtful. "Go ahead if your heart says so. Get a waçky person to crack this one. This is new—good humor hits harder than logic. But you need your Cyrus Broacha to crack this. As for me, I am looking forward to the fruition of this idea." I looked at him, and then he smiled, of all things, a warm, open smile.

"You don't want to take this up?" He asked.

"No way. You know I don't have a humour bone. I can end up dragging the whole concept down to logic and feelings." I grinned at him. Then he smiled, revealing dimples I could take a bath in. "But I can give you enough love to work on your idea, better it and see it to fruition," I added, shaking my head. His eyes widened.

"Ahh, and I thought you could take half the thinking part," he added, and I made a gesture to express my disbelief.

"By the way, I forgot to mention my mom is coming next week. Not that it is required to be mentioned here, but I would love it if we could go together to meet her." His eyes twinkled. Mine narrowed.

I was unable to contain the exuberance within.

He looked at me with a gay and cordial smile and a charming light in his eyes, and added, "I want to tell her about us. I know it's quite early, but I feel I should. I want her to know. Knowing her, I am assuming she will be supportive."

" I am sure she will be," I said calmly, placing my hand on his.

***

He was still engrossed in his work when I reached home. There was a spread of papers across the table. He loved working on paper while conceptualising something. It always seemed quaint to me; I could never quite get used to working that way.

"Do you know you are looking like a recovering alcoholic right now?" I teased.

"I have been busy working on an advertising concept for a sports drink," he breathed. His eyes looked hooded and heavy. A sharp nagging pain lanced through me, seeing him so wearied. That was his usual, to bury himself deep in thinking like this.

"I would love to listen to your concept if you wanna share that at this stage." I looked into his dark eyes. He was guileless, and that took my breath away. I knew I could adore him more than anyone and love him unconditionally. I would hold on, just as my sister had suggested.

I looked at him again and, unable to hold back, I leaned in and kissed him. I grabbed his face between my hands, pulling his lips to mine. I wanted to taste the moment, to feel his surprise melt into mine. Parting from myself, I hugged him tight and whispered 'I love you' in his ears. He breathed against my ears; I loved that warmth. I wanted to dissolve all the sullen feelings sunk between us. When I finally pulled away, I rested my forehead against his, smiling softly. The kiss had said everything I couldn't put into words.

I felt euphorically empowered. I dissociated and took a step back.

"Don't go, stay here for some time with me," he murmured. And he inched forward and buried himself in another passionate kiss, while my fingers twisted into his hair. I was restraining myself, but my desires unfurled with the same intensity. A stream of emotions blossomed inside me, which desired to be let out. I wanted to present all my compassion to him, assuming that would render his heart free.

He looked at me. So deep. I could notice the change in his looks, the hooded look waning and transforming into something desirable. He took my head in his hands and kissed me, long and hard, igniting my body and charging the flow of blood inside. I moaned as he kissed me. He was wilder than usual. The dark side of him was overpowering him and regaining its control, and I was letting this darkness flow out of him.

I reached for the second button on his shirt and heard him take a deep breath. His face looked relaxed, the remorse and wearied look had waned. I gently undid the button, and my fingers glided down to the next. His eyes had widened, large and luminous. He looked so beautiful, even when wrapped in his inhibitions, insecurities, and qualms. I placed a kiss on his chest and gently took off his shirt. His fair body glistened. I leaned forward and buried myself in him, my tongue exploring his chest. I made my intention clear, and there was a look of satisfaction in his eyes. He looked at me as I unzipped his pants.

"Take off your shirt too," he commanded in a low tone. In the next breath, he pushed me onto the bed and was over me, wrapping me in his arms, his hands claiming my body as he tilted my head back, exposing my throat to his hungry gaze. He kissed me passionately, as wild as I could have imagined him getting. There were no featherlight kisses - only deliberate moves to assert dominance. I could feel that darkness spill out of him, thick and undeniable. The romance was replaced by raw desire that consumed him entirely. I responded with equal fervour. He ran his lips down my body, slowly and claiming, nibbling my body softly, leaving love bites as flags of his conquests. A moan escaped me. I had longed for this unrestrained passion. Our bodies pressed close, his arousal firm and insistent against mine.

We rolled. I eased down and tugged his pants and boxers sharply. He grinned. He closed his eyes and surrendered to what he knew was coming next. I was hedonistic, liberated, and free to speak my desires loudly. Deep down, this was what I had always craved —not tender romance, but wild, untamed love. His darkness didn't frighten me; it came as a blessing, a mirror to my own hidden hunger.

"Fuck," he hissed and gently cradled my head and moved deeper inside my mouth. I had wanted this moment for a long, to take my boy and merge his being with mine. I emerged, scaled up his body, and wrapped myself like a vine around him. He tugged off my t-shirt and threw it carelessly on the floor. I was naked, wanting, and waiting. He looked at me, his look gentle and comforting. He smiled, his usual elegant smile, comforting, deep, and romantic. The darkness had lifted and in its place stood the old lover, the one who knew how to hold me tenderly. We spooned and kissed—feather-soft kisses that spoke of comfort, not conquest.

"Come inside me," I murmured against his lips. His eyes drank me in. He reached down, not taking his eyes off me. His dark eyes, his deep gaze. Something seemed held in that gaze, an age-old mystery, or a deep, buried desire.

"You are so gorgeous," he muttered. I tilted my head and beamed at him. He licked his lower lip and entered me. I took a deep breath, and soon pain melted into pleasure and a slow, consuming fullness took over me. In that moment, I felt him entirely —his darkness, his desire—and I felt content. I longed for this – wild desires melting into moments of poetic, quilted romance. I loved him in that moment, and in our shared smiles and lingering gaze, many unspoken promises bloomed.

***

"You didn't tell me about your advertisement concept, or sorry, perhaps I didn't give you the opportunity to tell," I said as we held each other in a warm embrace.

"I guess because we were in the heat of the moment. So, I am developing this advertisement for a friend. The product is a health drink, and I am adding a rainbow flavour to the advertisement."

"Interesting, fitting the rainbow concept in a health drink advertisement. Tell me more," I insisted.

"It's about a guy and a girl, both falling for this athlete guy, who is having this health drink. You will have to see the script and imagine the drama to understand it. Would you like to?" He murmured and kissed my forehead.

"I would love to." I smiled and shifted languorously beside him.

And the next moment, he narrated his concept. It was jovial, light, and equally progressive. His face was back to business, beaming as he waited for my reactions. Frankly, it worked on me like a fairy-tale: a grand concept, yet simple. Two people falling for the same guy, so routine, except that a girl and a boy fell for the same guy, that was novel. And he had blended this novelty with remarkable ease. The thought was sincere. I smiled at him and expressed my acknowledgement.

He was elated. His ad would be a new chapter in the Indian advertising industry. The ad could create a ripple effect. And many more creators would think of something similar and novel. That could blossom ideas in the conscience of society. I looked at him; he looked content and in harmony with himself.

Out, Proud and Loud

"Morning, baby," Dhruv whispered as he nuzzled my neck, and I slowly awoke. Bright early morning light flooded the room. He softly caressed my bare chest, gently teasing it. It had been almost two months with him and I had got accustomed to the rare breed of the naughtier him. He was usually the sane, poetic lover, more used to making love a piece of art, but seldom he turned into the rebel connoisseur. And he was trying to be at his rebel best that morning. It was more like shedding one skin to grow another. He wished me a 'good morning' again, his voice drifting in the haze of my half-waking mind, like a thread pulled from the fabric of a fading dream. A morning dream. I turned. He was smiling shyly at me, his dark eyes glinting with something mischievous. His hair was tousled, catching the morning light in unruly waves.

"Morning," I whispered as I rubbed my eyes and put my hands across his chest. I smiled back at him. "What is making you be in such a good mood today?"

He basked in some unknown bliss, almost like stretching his hands to the blue sky pointing at the horizon, imagining a golden table with friends around, savouring elysian bread, drinking

God touched wine and singing the last, almost forgotten songs from the countryside. He bent to kiss me and ran his fingers across my face. He held me in his gaze and clasped my face. We looked at each other and smiled, a groggy smile, and then he rubbed his nose against mine. I could see pure bliss in his eyes, the feeling that accompanies something pure and pulchritude. I could see fairies dancing in his eyes, tossing their gossamer scarves into the air—each one unraveling like a secret—while elves waited below, ready to catch them with reverent hands.I leaned to give him a return kiss, soft initially, becoming longer and more intense with time. We remained in each other's embrace for some time, kissing and adoring ourselves.

"Time we should get up. I already feel famished, and I am sure the breakfast is still to be done," I said, breaking the spell, we were in.

"Will you come to my house in the evening to meet my mother?" He asked.

"Is this the reason why you were so generously good?" I smirked teasingly. "Don't worry, I will. Who will not accept such a beautiful gesture?" I said softly. I got out of bed to prepare breakfast. Not sure of his plans, I asked, "Will you bring her to the workplace too?"

"No, that's not the plan. I don't want her to hog the limelight. People already see me differently—like I don't quite fit. I'm pretty sure they think I'm weird. And bringing my mom? She's too well-known. I'd rather not."

"Let me correct you here, they find you both weird and capable..." I answered before he could say a word further. "They find you a bit inaccessible, if I may put it that way. And to add to all that the favouritism you show towards me. I guess the corridor whispers have already started about us, you know, the usual gossip of high likeability of a guy being gay, if he spends a lot of time with a gay guy, " I murmured, amused, pouring milk in a bowl of granola. His eyes alighted with humour.

"And do you mind that?" He remarked. What an abstruse question, I thought.

"Why would I mind it? And anyway, the gossip is not about me; it's about you. I can return the question and ask you if you mind that," I answered.

He leaned back with a mock look of disapproval, but he knew I was right. This was all about him—and there was never an *us* in the whispers. I had a feeling he relished this undue attention, even if it was undeserved. And to an extent it made things easy for him, with people already having a fair idea of about him. And let's accept it, you don't come out to your office folks. That seems unnecessary, and seemed too out of line.

"Is it too early to ask you to settle down together?" His words were softer and conciliatory. I was amused how every conversation finds one focal point – settling down together.

"Settle down…that's like a surprise question…well, it's been just two months for us, and candidly we are deeper into our relation than what a two-month period holds. But settling down together requires a bit of more thinking. We can afford to give it some time. Some time to even know each other better. I mean more than this. And before that, my love boy, let us see how things go with your mom," I said in a calculated tone, swallowing my words and trying to bring it all together to remain coherent. I could sense his grin at the other end, he listened intently. I continued in my calculated tone, "Frankly, I am a little scared of the unwanted controversy it could lead to in workplace."

"You think it could?"

"Which same-sex love story hasn't? You think the people around us are mature enough to get that there is something beyond the man-woman binary? The straight in this country are really not straight in their head," I retorted, but mildly, expressing more despair than anguish.

"I get your anger," he said softly.

I offered him granola for breakfast. And I thought since the discussion had started, it was time for me to suggest something drastic, I was sure he wouldn't like it, but then it had to be said and pondered upon.

"Now that we are discussing the office place, you think it will be good for us if I take a different job in future? That way, we can escape a lot of unwanted nerves" I could hear my heartbeat fast when I said that.

"Oh, that's utter nonsense," he answered with genuine annoyance. "How come sometimes you act so foolish? What made you even think such a thing?"

"Nothing, just that I don't want this situation to get creepy for us." Honestly, I didn't have an answer to his question. Maybe I was wrong and foolish as he put it, or maybe I was just being over cautious.

"You are totally forgetting that I am not just a senior management here, I am also the shareholder. If anybody has issues with what happens inside the office and what two people do in their private lives, that person will see the door. And it's not because it's about me, but it is the right thing to do—respect people's lives and identity. Someone's life is not a matter of gossip."

I looked at him, his nervous lips, his pristine neck whose pureness spread to the extreme expanse of his chest, his deep, tremulous eyes. He was frowning. We cut short our conversation.

It seemed detached in time and space from our situation and from what we'd come to do. Either way, I had my answer. My fears had been assuaged. I consoled him that it was I who had to be cautious, or at least look cautious, every moment. I had acquired this trait and got used to it, and it was how I was born—the overthinker type, the genuine pessimist, who thought of himself as the conscious keeper, but was nothing more than a coward most of the time.

"Leave that thinking part to me…" he said with a hint of persuasion, and I gave him a weak smile which fell as quickly as it had come. I took that as a cue to say, 'this piece of conversation is over'.

"You need to think about the evening first, I am taking you to meet my mom and tell her about us, and that is bigger than all the office whispers combined, which, to put on record, haven't found a base to base themselves on," he added.

I looked at him, he held my hands, gently rubbing them, and a wide smile spread on my face. How silly I was to think of those worldly affairs when my world had condensed to that sublimely smiling face. A man who could hold me and say with his eyes that he valued me. A warm embrace where I could feel protected and loved.

Everything unfolded like the pages of a perfect love story. And if you believe in fairy tales, then yes—I was living one. While so many gay stories are marked with struggle —fighting against oneself, against family—I lived a fairy tale with my prince. Even the madness between us, has found a way to turn something strangely beautiful.

"And have you thought of how you are going to do that?" I asked, my tone subtle.

"Not so far. I tried to tell her once, to be honest, but couldn't devise a way. And since I was out of India then, and had no idea or plan to come back, I never tried to put many efforts in having a conversation with her. Now that I think of it…it could…as well…be an impromptu exercise. But somewhere, I am still thinking about it. Well, either way, the lady is heading for a big shock," he said amusedly.

"Hell, sure she is." I said rolling my eyes. I took a pause and then I added, "What does your intuition says about it?"

"Umm…. you know Anu, things were never so great between us. And we both live with a guilt that we never tried to understand each other. And though we have grown successful, personally we suffered quite a bit. I don't know her side of the story, and she doesn't know mine. But I have a strong feeling, she will be accepting of us. She does not want to lose me, that I am very sure of," his eyes gleamed as he said this. But I could feel the ache in his voice.

That was going to be a big day for him, and for us. Between our smiles, we knew the story could take a rough turn. A little voice in Dhruv's heart enthused him to do this. But truth always comes veneered with uncertainty. He inhaled the air, puffed out his cheeks and breathed it out between his protruded lips. I dropped my eyes and smiled a smile of approval, a genuine expression to state, and deep in my heart, the voice that resonated was— 'no matter what, I'll be with him.'

***

I arrived on time. Dhruv had been waiting, a flicker of anxious anticipation in his eyes. We had agreed to take things normally. I'd be introduced as a dear friend whom he had invited to dinner.

Only when the time felt right, and Dhruv had the courage, would he tell his mother. Until then, we were to play our parts. We had kept an option to not tell her that evening and wait for some opportune time in the future. But deep down, we both knew that there is never a better time than some awkward, unexpected moment to tell the truth. A part of me was not in favour of him opening up to his mother. And then a part was enthused about this. I was scared, confused, and probably desperately wanted to escape that unwelcome situation. But I was there—I had to be. There was no way out. Whether he chose to tell her or not, that was his decision to make, not mine.

Dhruv's mom, Melissa Shankar, was relaxing on a couch when I reached his home, turning pages of a lifestyle magazine. Dhruv came to get me —a half-hug, a smile full of confusion, and a muddled look on his face. I could sense his helplessness. His face wore the look of someone lost in a maze of emotions.

These are usually the best situations to open up, when you have reached the point of realisation that there was nothing you could have done differently. In those moments, you speak the truth, as brutal as it may be.

I looked at Melissa, an ageless grace, comfortable in her skin and grays, blooming, effervescent, and confident. She looked at us and stood to welcome me, wearing her buoyant, compassionate smile. Looking at her smile, I could easily guess what made Dhruv's smile so infectious. He had got his mother's personality, definitely her smile, and probably his father's looks.

My eyes fell on the west wall where stood a gigantic wall clock, its pendulum oscillating with a heavy, monotonous clang. This was a new addition to the list of classic furniture and earthy items Dhruv liked. The clock had brazen lungs, which I was certain made the sound both deep and musical. A loud thud of the clock, at that instant, could have calmed me. I was not ready for that evening; I wasn't ready when things opened in my family — how could I possibly be prepared for his? And in both moments, I had no plan, no script to follow. I looked at Dhruv and smiled — a quiet acknowledgment of our shared nervousness, of the quiet absurdity of it all. In that silent exchange, we made wordless vows to each other. And then the clock chimed. It produced the same emotion, the same disconcert and tremulousness, and meditation. It managed to break the eerie spell of self-doubt, pulling us back to ourselves.

I looked at Melissa, and she wore a comely smile. I wasn't sure of how Dhruv intended to open up, what moment he was waiting for, what context he had in mind. We had not discussed much. Just a simple 'I will take care of that' was his reply. I was certain that even he had no idea how he was going to open up. I expected it to be spontaneous, taking everyone by surprise, and not giving any chance to anyone in the room to contemplate much. All if it happens. I remembered the time when I had opened up to my mother. That was spontaneous too – no planning – not enough thinking. It was clear to me, like peering through some old, dusty windowpane; just a swipe of a hand, and the past could come flashing by with its unforgiving details. I could see it. Everything is so clear. Just that everything I had said then was blurred and indistinct, and yet painful.

"Mom, this is Anuj. I wanted you to meet him. I wanted to tell you that we love each other," came his blunt confession. That was more abrupt than I could have thought of. No context, no base, bang came the shot!!

I looked at him, and then my eyes shifted to Melissa. We haven't even greeted each other properly. She looked as shocked as I was. This was unplanned; instead, it seemed that he rejected the idea of planning. Her face turned white. There was an eerie silence set among us; our faces wore blank expressions. Nothing moved. The gigantic wall clock seemed to have gone still, holding time, and holding all the uncanniness of the moment.

"Won't you say something?" Dhruv asked in a low tone.

She looked at us again, her eyebrows lifting in quiet disbelief – a flicker of helplessness crossed her face. She was clearly taken aback by her son's revelation. "Dhruv, I know I wasn't there when you needed me. I should have given you more time, even when you were with me, but I never loved you less. I feel sad that I couldn't be the mother you wanted or deserved. But was I this bad that you held this truth from me for so long? Couldn't you ever trust me with your truth?" She said and took a deep breath.

Knowing a little bit of history between Dhruv and his mother, I could make a wild guess where the conversation was heading. It was difficult to say with certainty what was going on in her mind then. I had pictured her to be a complicated mind, as Dhruv was.

"I have no issues with your preferences, Dhruv. And I know you know this. I understand being gay is as normal as being straight. I am not worried about that. I am worried about what went so horribly wrong between us that my thirty-year-old boy could never tell his mother this…Did you think I'll oppose this relation?" She exclaimed. I breathed a sigh of relief. Dhruv's eyes beamed with content and appreciation.

"It often occurred to me that you owe truth and explanation, but I could never have the courage to state this." He blinked.

"You don't need courage for this," she said softly. "I've already lost too many moments with you to waste any more questioning your identity or your choices."

"I feel so relieved, Mom. And I am sorry I didn't trust you with my truth," Dhruv spoke as strings of tears rolled down his cheeks."

In the next instant, he stepped forward and wrapped his arms around his mother. And in that embrace, their tears washed away years of pain, disenchantment, and unspoken grudges. I stood there, beguiled, and wondered how different their low conversation, interrupted by genuine sobs of release, was from my own high-pitched, fractured exchange with my parents when I came out to them.

"I am sorry, Mom…for not trusting you, and thanks for understanding," Dhruv cried. There was a certain wealth in those tears, a wealth of gentility. Not everyone gets to live a moment like that. Some of us — like me — have to wade through a maze of heightened emotions just to stand in the light of our truth, our unchanging, undeniable truth. We live on conditional acceptance, dragging ourselves through the darks, lumbering the weight of our souls into forgotten corners.

"I wish you had shared this earlier. Nevertheless, I am happy for you. True love is always a blessing," Melissa replied, clasping her son's face in her hands.

"I know there are still many things we need to talk about — truths you've kept from me," she said, her voice warm and steady. "But I'll wait for the right time, for the moment you trust me enough to share them."

He was, and he knew. Even I didn't know how much he was keeping inside him and letting his fears feed on his psyche. I kept still and said nothing.

It was their day, and I wished—with all my heart—that tears could melt away every wrong. I wanted the darkness in him to finally let go. Inside the grown-up man he had become, a scared, petrified boy still lived — a boy who often surged to the surface, overwhelming the man meant to contain him. The man seemed too fragile, or perhaps too bound by fear, to resist. I longed for that boy to step into the light and reveal his face.

***

"It's still early," I said to myself, looking at the time on my mobile. A small smile spread on my lips as I snuggled further into the crinkled sheets, tugging at the blankets around my chest. Grumbling and still groggy with sleep, I pulled at the blanket to cover my shoulders properly. The blankets moved in compliance, and I let out a sigh of contentment. Those were to be my first winters with Dhruv, and winters are extraordinarily romantic.

Curling my body closer into the sheets, I frowned as the blankets slipped again. I wondered why, but was too drowsy to think and act. My fingers gripped a source of warmth; his hand lay heavily across my abdomen. I peeled open my lumber-leaden eyelids to discern where and how the blankets had snagged. My eyes followed the trail. It was the mischievous him, deliberately pulling the sheets. Blinking and confused, I snuggled against him, my dire attempt to not wake up and enjoy another hour of that wintery delight under the blankets.

The previous night had been heavy. Dhruv had spoken to his mother about our relationship, and as they hugged during the conversation that followed, I could feel that the warmth that was missing between them was finding its way back into their lives. And in those moments of compassion, darkness slithered away. His mother stood by him, unwavering. All she wanted was her son's happiness, regardless of where it came from or what form it took.

"You are so reckless," I whispered, voice quivering, my breath racing as I snuggled against him.

"I should leave you no choice other than loving me, even if that means being reckless," he whispered, cocooning me.

"What's making you go so larky in the morning? Is it the effect of that late-night chat with your mother? You came to the room after I had gone to sleep," I said, as my chest beat wildly in his embrace. I glanced around the room before settling my eyes on him. The dark wooden fan spun around, wobbling slowly and slightly, casting flashes of dark shadows that danced across the room, filtering the sunlight that slipped into the room through the white curtains.

"Hmm, tell me you missed me. It got really late catching up on all those lost years between us. But you know, it felt good." He smiled, a soft, contented smile.

"I can understand that. I am just curious what you people talk about? I hope I have that privilege to butt in your personal life," I spoke softly. A digital clock, perched over some old books, blinked 09:00 am in its red letters. Ah! Who cared…

"Nothing much! She asked me about us. General stuff like how and where we met, and then some old gossip. I realized there was so much we had to catch up on, like my life outside India, and then mostly our lives without each other—basically a mother-son life that had condensed to phone calls and chats. So much remained concealed in those talks. We regretted not being there for each other, mostly she, but I now realise it was my fault too," he said with a whisker of regret.

"I am sure you had your own reasons," I whispered, my eyes widening.

"Reasons or misunderstandings—what to call it? I am not so sure at this point. I wish I didn't have those and that I was able to trust her more and be there for her as she faced life. I felt sorry after yesternight's conversation with her that I could never see through my mother's struggles or ever appreciate how she succeeded in her endeavors against many odds. I was just too fond of her success and the luxury and independence it brought for me to look beyond that. I feel so bad about it now."

"Well, you people did have a long and deep chat. This sort of realisation can only come out of a true and empathetic conversation." I clasped his face in my hands. Drawing myself closer to him, I added, "I don't think you need to feel bad about it. I guess even she couldn't see your struggles as she battled hers. Sometimes we get too entangled in our lives," I consoled. We talked in short sentences. He nodded, sucked in uncontrolled amount of breaths and tears sprung to the corner of his eyes.

"I am glad she seemed pleased with our relationship. We didn't talk much about us last night, but I know she's supportive. And I am certain that in the days to come, she'll grow fond of you too," he wheezed, rubbing the tears from his eyes. His reaction was golden, content, and sanguine.

"I do wait for that day. I am so happy you have such a mother. You are the rare contented lot in this small community of the dejected lots," I said, a whiff of the discontent with my own family wearing down in my voice.

"Hasn't this been a little teary-weary morning? A little heavy for the senses. Can we just pull the quilt over us and make it a little more memorable?" He said teasingly. I winked and chuckled, pushing down the ill feeling swirling in my stomach.

***

Pulling on a fresh set of clothes, I stepped down, where Melissa was waiting for us for breakfast. My stomach was rumbling at the thought of her reaction. My hair was still a mess, and my heart a beat or two away from infarction. I quietly hummed to myself to keep the unwanted thoughts away. She gave me a welcoming smile. I managed one myself, a bit unsure smile, one coming more as courtesy than genuine.

"Dhruv is getting ready; he will take some more time," I said in a balanced tone, holding back my words.

"Not an issue, you can come and wait with me. I hope my choice of breakfast suits you."

I looked at the lavish display on the table —sandwiches with mashed avocado at one end of the table, fresh juice on the other, a literal choice of eggs, and bowls of granola cereals with cut strawberries. This family certainly lived in style.

"We could hardly talk last night. Dhruv mentioned you wished to meet me. Well, he mentioned quite a lot of things about you. So I was both excited and intrigued to talk with you," she said, making a genuine attempt to strike up a conversation.

My stomach was aching, and I was trying to pump some maturity into myself. The truth was, I was feeling a bit out of place. I had wanted to go back to my house the previous night, but Dhruv insisted on my staying back. And seeing how emotive my man could get, I chose to stay back. The awkwardness I felt was rooted in the social dilemma I had been wrangling with; a mother had just learned her son was gay, and now his partner stayed back for the night. In an ordinary circumstance, that alone might have felt like too much, too soon. I took a deep, self-consoling breath.

"I admire your work. I believe everyone does, but then not everyone gets a chance to know you personally. We even studied your early work in our college. Dhruv did mention his mother many a time, but I had no idea it was you he was referring to. I got to know that just a few weeks back, and I was like…Yeah, I don't know, I don't have exact words for my reaction," I answered, my words a little slurred and incoherent.

"Surprised, maybe…" she hinted

"Some more than that — but something on those lines," I replied. She chose to smile, a smile of appreciation.

"Dhruv can hide a lot. I have always known that. Honestly, I didn't know how to act yesterday because I wasn't expecting that. To be true, I never expected him to be in a relationship, after his last one…"

"He never really talked about his past relationships… he never brought them up, and I guess I never asked," I said, a hint of curiosity in my voice. "I, too, have little idea, except that he was in a relationship. I never knew it was a boy he was with, and I never sought much information. As usual, I left it to him to decide when and how to disclose that to his mother. I always wanted him to believe that his mother stands by him. Probably he does now, and that is comforting to me," she spoke in her usual calm voice. There was an uncanny calmness in her, a sort that can make you introspect. Perhaps it was a consequence of the tempestuous life she had lived.

I looked at her. She held a deep, penetrating gaze, seeking more answers. "He had depression episodes in his pre-teen days. I took him to the therapist. He didn't say a word to me or the therapist. He was badly scared or deeply scarred. I had always remained quite concerned for him, but I could never make him feel that…" She took a breath and continued, "Soon after we left India and moved to Paris, where, little by little, he began to live a more normal life. For a mother, that was more than what she could have sought. I never tried to investigate the reasons for depression, thought it's better to keep the lids closed than open it and let the unholy spell out. Or perhaps, I was too ill-equipped to handle that situation," she said, her voice choking out of motherly concern. I was aghast at how much weight the woman beside me had to carry, and yet she never lost control of her life. Only a woman is capable of managing that.

"I know fragments of what happened with him. I also never tried to inquire further. I agree with you, these are wounds of the past, and they better remain buried. If and when he wishes to open up, he will have my ears. Don't worry, I love him, and I won't leave him," I said, each word separately.

"I am pleased he chose you." Those words meant a lot to me. Having taken almost two years to come to terms with my parents on my identity, those words meant heaven to me. We smiled at each other, seemingly seized by the same idea, and hurrying towards a convergence point. And it was like a lifetime of emotions wrapped in those six words.

"Candidly, I wasn't expecting things to be this gentle, and his idea of telling you had me worried," I confessed, and she smiled while putting some fresh fruits on my plate. "If I'm honest with you, I live with this fear of falling in love, having it all, and then losing it. It has happened before, and it was devastating. I want everything to go fine with Dhruv, and I am ready to go to any extent to see that it goes fine," I added.

She looked at me as she passed on the plate of fruits, and then with a calm look on her face, she answered, "Leave that part to him, I know he is good at bringing balance to things. Let us just play our parts as honestly as we can, not doing anything more or extraordinary. He is a pacifist of sorts. He will remain balanced in all troughs and bends of life. As a mother, I can tell you Dhruv is way more sophisticated than he appears."

Dhruv came down. "Are you guys catching up on something in my absence?" He cried, and coming close, he hugged his mom and avoided hugging me in her presence. I merely rolled my eyes and hummed at his response, though a smile tugged at the corners of my lips in response to his ridiculous question. He gave me a soft smile and took a seat beside me.

"Yes, we were catching up on things. And there was so much catching up to do with someone I grew up reading about and took as my inspiration. So, as they say, when you see a river, you must follow the source. And lo, lucky me, I am basically at the source. So I used this time and opportunity to know more about your mom's work, take a shot at impressing her a bit, and to know more about you," I mumbled. They smiled.

He fixed himself a plate of poached eggs on toast, a sandwich on one side of the plate, and coffee. Melissa looked at him, grey-haired with mouse bright eyes, looking hardly a shadow of an inspiring lady, I knew, looking more a troubled mother giving her son smiling reassurance that all was safe in their dear tiny world, and probably eager to give heartbreakingly insecure snugness.

The previous night, I realised how little I knew of Dhruv. My soft prince reduced to an expression of loss, as he snuggled in his mother's arms and cried. A river of tears, I presume. They talked while I waited impatiently in the room, often coming out to listen to their incoherent conversations; wondering if he told her what scared him — the episodes of child abuse and how he overcame that, and what demons still lay in him.

When he came, he looked reduced to an expression of longing defeat, with a dull, harassed stare, a coarsened, deep voice, a mouth dragged down into a grimace, and cheeks sagging, bogged down by sacks of their own toxins. There were no questions to be asked or explanations to be given. I stared at a creature struggling to crawl out of its dark den. There was no alternative to that struggle. It lived in him.

As I stared into him, I saw many faces, except for the face I knew. I saw the face of a child, a growing boy, a teen, a young man, and a not-so-young man. They all lived there, like fossils of some archaic time—their impressions dark and palpable. The present didn't require its past. And still the present looked afraid of that past, the fossilised past that had long gone?

"I wanted to ask what keeps you busy these days. I learnt from some people that you have taken a break from advertising and were planning to establish something," I asked Melissa to break the eerie silence that had set in among us.

"Not exactly given up. Advertising is in my blood. If I don't make ads, I am not Melissa Shankar. You may say things are slow these days, as most of the time goes into my new venture. The idea is in the nascent stages, you may say, at a blueprint stage, but a good share of mind-work has gone into it. It takes a lot of my time. I still dedicate some time to my advertising firm. I have realized Mad House can't run without my madness. I have been asking Dhruv to take over Mad House, but now I know why he was so reluctant to leave the FM channel. Perhaps sometime in the future, I hope he makes up his mind to go mad at Mad House. Or probably you can join him there, that will surely keep him in Mad House," she answered teasingly, and I couldn't hold my grin, and Dhruv showed his displeasure at being teased.

"Frankly, I'll let Dhruv decide that. I don't think I have much problem shifting to Mad House. I'd be rather happy working with you, and learning from the advertising giant," I chuckled, and then continued, "…and I hope you won't mind me asking more about your new venture, I am just curious."

"Oh no! You don't have to even give a second thought to that. I am working on starting a lifestyle magazine, which has, sort of, been a dream project for me. I always wanted to do that and always felt the need for a good lifestyle zine in India. I see a lot of space in the lifestyle market of India, where I can tuck myself with ease. And that made me reconsider, prompting me to take a break from the advertising business and invest my time here instead," she added.

"I don't know much about the market, but the idea definitely is striking. You keep challenging the creative side of yours…" I said in an appreciative tone, squealing happily.

Dhruv busied himself with breakfast, his eyes ripped away from his mother. I could feel a recognisable uncanniness between the two. Why had he not told his mother about his childhood trauma? Why could he never be that open with her? I wished I could understand instead of being so inordinately contemplative of the situation. Oh, why do such thoughts and expressions flood me in the morning, like spasms of some unanticipated realization? The morning spasms had always been so painful to treat.

I tried, but it was almost a disastrous failure to convey my remarkable lack of understanding of the insubstantiality of the relation those two individuals shared. They seemed appreciative of each other, at times holding each other in high regard, yet it was easy to sense the unease that hung between them.

Breakfast with Dhruv was usually the best time of the day. Those were meant for soulful conversations over coffee. And we talked about everything under the sun. Our conversations had an abstract starting point and an abstracter ending.

Dhruv and his mom sat in some awkward silence, in expectation of the other person initiating a random topic to break that silence. I wondered if those two were the same people who had a long, deep conversation the previous night. A span of ten hours, and they sat there like strangers, bound by serendipity but unwilling to know each other.

I could guess a silent tension between them. A tension that is not circumstantial, but something that has developed over time. It was a figment from their past. It was something unspeakable, yet well-preserved. It wasn't something that you could nail with a word; it was lodged deep within them, coated with a feeling of distrust, and an enormous amount of rage and shame.

Every moment I looked at them, I felt a strange feeling, as if their hearts wanted to reconcile, but something held them back. They respected each other, no doubt, but they couldn't absolve each other of the crimes they had committed against each other.

"You are surprisingly silent, Dhruv," I said softly.

"Nothing like that. Just nothing much to say,"

"Will you drop me off at my house after breakfast? I have certain things to attend to, and I had better let you two catch up." I smiled a reassuring smile. I wanted some air, and just so suddenly, I started feeling a misfit in that house. Dhruv nodded and hummed a low 'yes'.

The Past Stung

It took me some time to push away my unsavoury thoughts and focus my attention on my life, after a rough and distracted start to the morning. I looked at him as he drove, his dark brows creased into a straight line, hair messed up with a few strands falling over his impossibly bright eyes. There was a feeling of escape caught in the gleam of his eyes. We didn't speak to each other on our way to my house, and then he spoke upon reaching, "Would you mind if I insist on staying back for some time?"

I chuckled at the thought of that. He never had to ask that. "Come upstairs," I said. "I've noticed you are a different person in front of your mother, sometimes abstruse and at times empathetic. It's so difficult to understand," I mentioned, pleading mentally, my eyes flickering between his forehead and bosom. He looked at me, a penetrative gaze looking for a benediction. "You still hold her culpable? You haven't been able to absolve her," I sighed softly. I know that wasn't a good time to say that, but I am just an uncontrollable mess.

I took a few steps towards him, embracing him in a comfortable half-hug. I asked, "Do you wish to talk about it?"

"I told you, Anu, it's an incident of child abuse," he answered, his reluctance evident on his face as a devilish reminder of how much he wanted to escape his past, and it was so clear that his mother was a part of that past. Every interaction with her took him closer to that past.

"It's not just an incident, Dhruv, you are petrified. And it's obvious on your face. I can easily get that it's way bigger than something being labelled an accident," I gulped as he let out an exhausted sigh and crossed his arms over his chest. He pried open one eye and gave me a withering look.

"What?" He asked, his voice deep and gruff.

"Please, trust me," I said softly. "You don't have to carry it alone—tell me what's on your heart."

"What do you want to know, Anu? And why?" His voice trembled with something between weariness and defiance. "Can we go back in time and undo it? Can your soft, sweet words heal those scars, or the anguish that scares me, and doesn't let me sleep at times?"

He paused, his eyes distant. "What do you seek even? To explore the depths of my soul to see how I survived loneliness, alienation, and loss?"

He took another pause. "And how do I even tell you this? I love my mother...I do, but it just hurts to remember that she wasn't there when all that happened. That she never tried to know what had happened?" There was a note of deep agony in his tone, a quiet ache that lingered just beneath the words.

"She always wanted to know. It was your reluctance and fear that she stopped exploring. She was scared that her trying to prod might break you. She even took you to a therapist. She acknowledges the fact that you grew up a troubled child. So, stop blaming her. You were too scared to tell her, and you still are scared. Let that fear go for once and face it." My tone was bellicose.

Dhruv had that nerve-crawling sensation that could not be removed by a smile or a hug. It was a realisation. His eyes moved hurriedly from me to the couch, and then from the couch to me: a brazen attempt to avoid me. His face became tense, his mouth tightened and twitched, lips pressed together in a grim line, and eyelids contracted nervously. Though his body remained in a perfect, relaxed posture, his expressions had changed. It seemed a separate identity existed in him, an identity that was an embodiment of his fears and darkness.

There hung a nervous silence between us.

A shudder passed through me as I grasped the weight of his silence—a silence that clung to him like a second skin, almost like a gentle hypnosis he'd long surrendered to. And in that moment, I realized what it might mean for us.

Before me stood a man vanquished in every phase of life—scars etched from a tormented childhood, a teenager haunted by fear and loss of his lover. His fears trailed him like shadows. He could never truly make peace with life. He looked at me, almost shrinking under the weight of the truths he held.

I went close and hugged him, a consoling hug. Inside, my broken man reeked like a rotten corpse.

***

And every night brought with it a forbidden tale of horror. I often wished I could vanish—become an eremite cloaked in shadows, leaving a frail trail, too hard to find or follow. What happened that day didn't stop there. It took different forms and became more regular. Even though I knew how it had hurt me, I could never give myself permission to label it as sexual violence. Possibly that's why I could never tell anyone about it; as a man, I didn't think I could be a victim or a survivor. I didn't think I had the right to say it. Sometimes in the dark of the night and during the sleepy afternoons, she would enter my room, and I would be ordered to go through an ordeal, an impassable, unforgettable episode of terror, leaving every time a huge, indelible imprint on my psyche.

We cannot solve a problem if we do not recognise its existence. My mother failed to understand, even when I tried my best to explain it to her. I wish she could have just understood that there was something wrong and tried to inquire more. My grandma was too frail with her disease and indifferent in her attitude. In that big house, with only three souls inhabiting its quiet spaces, even the corners seemed to hold their own shadows. My suffering got woven into the fabric of my day-to-day life. The face of her identity— simply that she was a woman—blurred my understanding, made it harder to name what was happening, harder still to step outside and ask for help.

I became silent and withdrawn, and there was no one to read those signs of change in me. My grades in school dropped, and no one noticed that. I felt helpless as day after day she came and touched me, kissed me, stripped me naked, all to make a man out of me. I hated the layer of skin I was clothed in. I looked into the mirror and hated the deep, dark eyes she so adored. I abjured the hands she took to her naked breasts, or the fingers she guided to her vagina. I began to believe the world had contaminated me and scrubbed myself clean to get rid of that contamination. I washed my hands and possessions like a maniac just so I could lose my fingerprints and sense of everything I was made to touch and go through. I cried as I sat below the shower, draped in soap and desperation. The contamination would not go. It clung to me, deeper than skin. It was perpetual, meant to stay in me like a scar.

"The sweetness in you is so seductive, it draws me to you," she whispered in my ear as she guided her hands under my pants. She stroked me while I looked haplessly into her eyes, my expression blank, my sensations dead.

First, I resisted, then I learned to comply. Resistance was futile; it only led to more hurting, more embarrassment: more abuses, taunts, and sometimes whips. She would call me names, and I helplessly listened. She asked me to smile, and I smiled, while quietly telling myself that this too would pass, that maybe one day the weight behind it would lift. She would guide me on how to lay, touch her, or take her, and I complied. I had random Kafkaesque visions, and my life was reduced to those experiences and visions. Nothing else existed—the rolling hills, the meandering roads, the vast expansive tea estates losing out to the woods or the splendid hill life—nothing mattered.

My grandma had gotten least concerned about me or my mother. She existed as a frail, old, grumpy lady with a huge estate to her name. My mother probably waited for her death to inherit the wealth and restore her sinking business. Everyone had their priorities, and I was never one of them.

"I want you to stay in Darjeeling with your grandma till things get easy for us here. The place is good. I am certain you will love being here," she said, condensing her motherhood into a curve of a smile. I obliged, as I always did with everyone. And I obliged till I was made to question my realities.

"You will grow into a sweet man, and when girls look at you and drool at your charm, don't forget your first love who showed you all the tricks and made you the man you are," her voice said quietly, a yelp escaping her lips as I scooted away from her. She untied her bra.

Her fair-complexioned body glistened. She took off my shirt. That day I fucked her hard, the way she wanted, the way she commanded me to. She hurled abuses at me while I fucked her, moaned with delight and dug her nails in my back. She moaned at the thought that her sweet child had attained his manhood. I hated myself as I gave in to her impish games. I conformed unwillingly, but I did that. And with every moment, every movement, self-loathing grew deeper. I betrayed myself, and I knew it.

The next day, I searched the shelves of libraries and bookshops for reassurance that what was happening to me was wrong. All the books described a male perpetrator —usually much older—preying on a young girl. I closed the book, invalidated. I stood there thinking who would believe me, and then what I did to escape all the shame, complying with her; didn't that invalidate all that I believed in? There was no easy belief in my story, that wasn't what violation looked like.

"Didn't I always say you have to learn to love it, and you cried like a sissy then. I kept insisting because I love you. I care for you. Who else does? Your grandma hardly cares, she never even enquires about you, and your mother isn't willing to even keep you with her. And isn't it good that you are here? You are getting all the love that a sweet boy like you deserves. And see, even you have started loving it. Getting better every day. All you ever needed was to love it."

I coughed uncomfortably. Sucking in a strained breath, I steeled my nerves to speak. "I can never like this." That was probably the first time in months when I had spoken anything more than 'leave me alone' or 'spare me'. She smiled, rubbing her face with her hands, fatigued. Her expression in an instant changed to a blank stare, eyes wide open as she looked at me with an odd expression. Her annoyance shone on her face. The young kitten had developed claws…

Things were never the same since that day. She knew she could control me, and she knew how to. She also knew I had no support. She was as vindictive as she was dominant. I was certain I would be shown my place after that rare show of strength. I knew she wouldn't harm me, but I feared something far more terrifying might happen instead. The timid boy in me was gone, and she could sense it. Her convulsion, annoyance, and repulsion became more visible. In a matter of a few days, I could see how easy it was to break out of that bondage. But grief only changes shapes; it never ends. A fourteen-year-old was no match for her desire for supremacy. If the control is not by default, you manipulate it. She wanted a vicious, stultifying control over my body, my emotions, and my psyche. And she would settle for nothing less.

I could see the signs of traumatic stress on my face in the mirror. In the marks on my body, I could realise the breach of my bodily autonomy, and in my deep eyes I would face my shattered dreams—I would stand there for hours, staring at myself—a spectre of loss, an artifact of sorrow, an undeclared loss.

"You are not some weird mess. You are a piece of my destiny, and you know how much I want you. When everyone pushed you to the edge, I came for you. I remained with you. I gave you everything you needed and deserved—love, attention, security—all because I love you and will always be there for you," she said as I shook my head, and she gripped my forearm tightly.

I could read her words, but I had no name for it. She showered me with sustained attention, a feeling I had always yearned for. She protected me from the bullies at school and sheltered me from the indifference that had become the constant feature of my grandma. Her attitude towards me was rare among the distracted shards of oneness and solidarity I was exposed to by my known ones. But she broke me. I feared her. I hated her. And slowly, I began to hate myself for staying close to her, for not knowing how to walk away.

Standing in front of the mirror, I could feel a part of me fumbling before her, towards a foregone possibility of security and happiness, oblivious of the mounting evidence of her acts and my unheralded rage towards her. How could I let her swallow me? I could no longer respect the attention she bestowed on me. I was laden with shame and guilt. And when plunged deep into those obnoxious thoughts of self-hatred and guilt, I started failing on other ends. I stopped calling my mother. Daily calls turned to alternate days, and then to weekly. Almost every time I told her I was happy, when I could have spoken the truth. I did break down sometimes, but those moments became less frequent with time. That shame and guilt broke me from within; it made me so helpless that I couldn't even ask for help.

Her damages did not leave scars, except for those on the psyche. She said she loved me, she saw my qualities and my weaknesses, and that she would shape me into someone who could overcome those weaknesses. At times, she said she desired me, and that she would keep me safe, and grow old with me. At times, she would come into my room and sleep beside me, slide her hands under my clothes, and whisper into my ears, "You don't even know how good you are."

Sometimes, she pitied me for being so weak to get bullied in school. She sympathised with me as I was alone and ridiculed me for being so unwanted in everyone's life. She told me I am not sexy, but she would have sex with me and let the man in me take over the boy. She kissed me, saying that I gave her pleasure and abused me for not being man enough. She would nurse me when I would hurt myself, and make me loathe myself for not being able to protect myself.

I knew I was navigating a crystalline, devastating landscape with bare feet, exposed, each step a quiet shatter beneath me. I couldn't say a thing to anyone. Who would believe me? Who was there to believe me? I often wondered if what I was living through was something unusual—something that didn't quite fit the script of suffering I'd read about. Sometimes the whole act ached deeply: she would hiss at me, abuse me, even beat me. Destiny can enslave even the brightest. I maintained a disordered silence, enduring the pain without protest.

Being left alone 'was the scariest realisation and the clumsiest of experiences. Even as a young boy, I had felt I had lived eternity, and probably I was dead inside. The boy existed, but the innocence had died. Sometimes I failed to contain the anger within. I would run to desolate corners and spend time hiding in random places where no one could identify me. I felt like a blackened slate, and I rejoiced in that slow death of what a life could be. The sane might have thought I was going insane—but having been pushed to the very nadir of my being, I began to see life differently. I started to understand its depth—and its hollowness. Life was nothing but an open field, vast and unstructured, where people played roles they were never meant to play, trapped not by their fate, but their reactions.

***

"You aren't the first fallen stone of an avalanche, Dhruv. You need to open the lid and release that horror off you. We are all victims of some form of abuse outside our cultural conversation. We all go through bad episodes. The reality is grim for many of us. We hop from one pool of abuse to the other, traverse from one tragedy to the other. But you can't live holding it inside you. One conversation that night, and you turned into a scared child. Or just see your relationship with your mom – it's even difficult to define it," I said, my tone carrying a hint of my uncontrollable frustration, my hands clasping his face, looking deep into his eyes to offer a facsimile of comfort.

"I was sexually abused…not once or twice, but for almost two years. Every day!!" he said in a low tone and immediately broke down in my arms. I stood flummoxed as he wept on my shoulders. I had no words or expressions to respond. In my embrace, I tried to shield my lover from the storm of contempt rising within him, holding him close, as if my arms could silence what his heart refused to forget.

As slowly as he could, he walked towards the sink. He opened the tap and splashed some water on his face, all with a degree of reluctance and unease. His face had turned pallid, his breaths were heavy, carrying a hint of fear. The room was wrapped in absolute silence. In that moment, we existed in a strange, fluid state where clarity didn't promise understanding, where falsehood could easily masquerade as genuine, and sensibility had been so ruthlessly challenged that it no longer felt like a refuge.

He had finally laid bare the truth that had lain buried in his bosom for years. The horror had come out, and in his eyes, I could find the frail, scared, young boy stepping into his teens, trying to decipher the abuse he was going through. His body was never truly his own. His emotions were crushed before they could be shaped, and he endured it all alone. There was no one to complain to or share with. Monsters are real; sometimes they surround us, sometimes they reside in us. It had been born in him, feeding slowly on his confidence, corroding sensibility, and eroding his sense of morality.

For half an hour, we did not speak a word. I had no words. I demanded no explanations; he didn't owe any. I just held his hand and cocked his head on my shoulders. I let my eyes speak, and his listen. Soon his tear-splattered cheeks dried, the pallid face regained its colour, but his soul had been trounced.

"And you hid this for all these years," I said lowly, each word distinct. I knew I could never step into his shoes; empathy was too small a word to understand what he had gone through.

He hummed softly, his eyes dropping down to where my hands were gently wrapped around his arm. I followed his gaze and let out a quiet hum, giving him a reassuring squeeze.

"We will fight this together. You are not alone henceforth," I spoke softly. But I knew it was his battle, and he alone had to fight that and overcome.

We can never comprehend this world. We can only learn that there are some dangers. And there are secrets. Some of these secrets bring release and redemption, and some unleash horrors, unimaginable and uncontrollable. His secret belonged to the latter.

All around him, I could see his world quietly falling apart as he spoke—unraveling with each horror he unearthed, each truth he had kept buried for so long. He had lost a part of himself long back and survived by clinging to the pursuits of his schedules — his immense reading, impassioned arguments, and concoctions of a fantasy world he wove to escape the realities that haunted him. He was burdened by his past. Something inside him had withered, quietly and irreversibly.

"What are we going to fight—the past that can't be changed?" He asked in a low, deep, and dying tone. "Or my lost childhood, or those fears that haunt me. I think I'm past that. I have learned to live with it. It has shaped me the way it could, and there's no more damage that can be done. And honestly, I am done fighting my fate." I listened to him, transfixed. I had no words…

That guy, grown quite unrecognisable by then, looked hardly an image of the one I had met and fallen in love with. We spent that evening talking about everything that came to our heads—mostly the sombre feelings. As we discussed, we realised both of us were prisoners of our past, and in countless and unrelatable ways, we were similar to each other.

But that day planted a fear in me — a scary thought of losing him. When you love someone that deeply, there is always a part of you that lives in fear, aching at the very idea of their loss.

***

"Do you know who Dephny D'Souza is?" I asked, my voice vibrating through me. I had asked Melissa to meet me in a nearby café. There was a LONG discussion pending.

"Yeah, I do. She used to work at our estate and used to look after my mother as her caretaker. I am not so sure, but she wore many hats there, from being the estate caretaker to managing many other small managerial tasks," she answered, still unruffled by my blunt question.

"Yes, she wore many hats, and one of those was of a child molester. She molested Dhruv for over two years, until the time he left that place," I said, my head straight, my eyes red with rage.

"That's impossible—she cared for him. Both Dhruv and my mother had said it time and again."

"I don't know these dynamics or what conversation he had with you. I believe in what he told me this morning. And trust me, I have never seen him this lost and broken. And that's what made me ask for this urgent meeting. I felt I had to tell you—someone had to, and bring that woman to justice." Dead silence. She had turned shamefaced, a realisation of how she had failed as a mother.

"That bitch!" She exclaimed angrily.

"I can get how angry you are. I am no less. I know you care about him, and I swear I won't rest until that woman pays for what she's done," I said, my voice low and trembling.

"I don't know where she is now. We sold a part of our estate and used that money to settle down and start Mad House. The rest was leased out. And since her services were no longer required, I asked her to leave. I helped her get a job in a bank. I haven't heard from her since," she said, her voice distant, still trying to absorb the weight of the truth.

"I'm completely with you on bringing her to justice. But for that, we will need evidence. And Dhruv will have to give an official statement. Only then will we be able to pursue the case." She spoke. I wondered how she could be so rational at that moment. Maybe she had buried it all as bygones, or maybe she was simply too weary to fight anymore. I, on the other hand, was failing to fathom the loneliness of my lover. I was determined.

"We can try to find her. But I can't forgive her. You haven't seen Dhruv break down—I have. And trust me, it's been the most harrowing experience of my life. It was scarier and more painful than anything I have felt before in my life," I answered, my eyes brimming with tears.

"I agree with you. If this can undo any of the wrongs done to my child, we should do this. I fear it won't, but I am still willing to go along with what you think. She is a sexual predator and a threat to many young minds," she answered.

"I shall use my contacts in the Darjeeling police to trace her. But I will advise you to keep Dhruv out of it until we have some information to build our case on. As you have seen, he has a lot inside him, and he takes time to heal. I knew something had hurt him; I could feel that and did everything I could to know that. He never told me, and so, after a time, I stopped insisting. Therapy helped calm his mind, but I could feel deep down that something remained, and even a figment of what remained was scary. I was scared to even touch that," she added in a low tone.

"I truly appreciate the bonhomie and love between you two: to share one's gravest pains, and to be able to feel and empathise with your lover's pains; that is the first sign of a strong relationship." She smiled, putting her hands on mine. "I am pleased that my son has someone like you who cares for him."

"Your words are appreciated," I replied.

"Do me a favour! Ask him to forgive his mother. I got so caught up in my own troubles that I failed to see how his innocence was being bruised. I could never be the mother he needed me to be. I feel sorry that he had to navigate through these hardships alone," she said, her voice thick with emotion as her eyes became wet.

"It would be wrong of you to blame yourself. You tried to do what you could. And it would be more wrong to argue on this with logic. You had no idea of what was happening with him." I gave her consoling looks and continued, "We can, however, put our energies into finding that monster."

"I shall do that; some phone calls might work." She placed her hand on mine. A gentle, motherly touch.

Little but Not Less

No matter how busy we were in our lives, Dhruv and I had developed a tradition of having Sunday breakfast together. And while Melissa had taken to reaching out to her contacts in Darjeeling to find Dephny D'Souza, I focused on staying close to Dhruv and comforting him. Not that he needed it, but I felt it was necessary. One week had passed since we had talked about the horrors that stayed with him. Though he refused to accept, I knew I had torn open an old wound, and I had no words to soothe his aching heart.

I could gauge that in his reclusion at work. He resisted nearly every established existing business norm, and the usual zeal he had for his work was missing. He wasn't him. He had grown frozen and withdrawn. The wound was deep and unhealed. It had lived in him for years, in every breath and move he took. His reluctance, anxiety, and even the milder shades of paranoia I could see, were ominous signs of a complete emotional breakdown.

He tried keeping up with his usual self, especially when around me, but that brightness was fleeting, while the loss he carried was enduring. As Melissa and I talked, Dhruv had bumped from one episode of loss to the other, and he kept all that to himself. She was right about him – his instinct was always to bury his emotions. That didn't solve anything. The feelings remained within, never finding their precipice and never releasing. The loss remained and grew deeper inside him.

"You haven't been yourself this week," I said, making a whining face to fake my displeasure.

"Is it? I'm sorry you felt so; that wasn't the intent. I, on the other hand, feel so drowned in work." He didn't have to explain.

"I guessed so. And that's why I eagerly waited for this Sunday to spend time with you. We spend less time together now," I said, eyes hopeful as I tenderly tugged on his sleeve.

He smiled. "I can actually smell comfort here," he sniffled, before squeezing my arms lightly. "Seems you have brought some changes to the balcony…" he said, stepping out.

"Not much, just got new plants and some more art pieces to fill the spaces."

"You love filling spaces…" he exclaimed, amused.

"And you leave them unfilled," I answered softly.

He turned his eyes towards me to gauge the gravity of the sentence. I took his hands in mine.

"Then I think I can entrust you with that task," he said as he held my hands and kissed them. After thinking for a moment, he leaned forward, his face centimetres away from mine. I could easily smell the heady perfume he was wearing. I gulped, my body arching backwards to move.

"Sssh... what are you doing, all my neighbours can see," I said, averting my eyes from him. "We should head inside," I murmured. He chuckled, gripped my chin, and his eyes dropped to my lips. My smile conveyed my approval.

"You have such drunken eyes," he said, pausing in front of me, eyes narrowed, lips curled. I let out an amused smile. "Be honest, have I been bad to you lately?" He asked an innocuous question, I must admit.

"Nope. I don't even know what made you think so. You have been tired lately. And what's so bad that a good hug or kiss can't repair," I said, hiding my pleasure in an amusing smile, rubbing the bridge of my nose. He smiled at my offer and willingly heeded my words. I was right, there really is no problem a good hug can't soften, if not solve.

"I'm fine," he whispered in my ear. I bristled and stumbled backwards. The back of my legs hit the frame of the bed, sending my legs folding and my body falling. His strong hands tried to grip mine as I fell, but my weight ended up dragging both of us down. I let out a laugh at the incident. The stumbling had brought him over to me.

I opened my eyes to see his dark eyes staring at me. His arms trapped my head between them, and I held him by his waist. His hair fell around my face. I loved it as his silky hair brushed my face. His legs tangled with mine at the edge of the bed. My hands rose upwards, fingertips brushing over his cheeks. A drooping smile sat on his face. I cherished the stillness of the moment, as if time itself had slowed just for us, to let us live it fully. There was a unique freshness in every moment.

He wrapped his arms around my back and buried his head in my neck, giving me soft kisses, nibbling my neck. It was always nice pressed against his body, and I loved the warmth of his skin. "I love you," I mumbled.

"I know you do," his voice vibrating through me as he whispered close to my ears. He looked at me, an expectant gaze and brushed his hands on my face. My lips parted to accommodate him. Some loose strands of hair fluttered against my eyelids; I closed my eyes. He slid his hands under my shirt, and his lips pressed against mine. The slight coolness of the moment made me flush.

We poured our pains and intimacies into each kiss, our chests bumping with every laboured breath. When he pulled away, he'd look down at me with a faint smirk and those deep, unreadable eyes.

"You okay?" He asked, and I nodded. He smiled a little. Leaning down, his fingers tangled in my hair, he pressed his lips against mine, and I sighed, melting into the warmth of that intent kiss.

I raised my arms, allowing him to take off my shirt. He took off his shirt, his body glistening against the backdrop of the sunlight filtering in through the curtains. My eyes roamed the expanse of his skin. I had never wanted him more than I did in that moment. I realised how much of myself I had been holding back to fit the softness he needed. But catching a glimpse of wildness in him stirred something deeper and aroused more intimate feelings in me.

I watched him in awe as he unzipped his denims. He came close, captured my face in his hands, and kissed me hungrily. Our tongues rolled, and he found an opportunity to stroke against my dorsum. I moaned as our tongues pushed and pulled, my teeth often tugging on his lower lip, making him groan in my mouth. I felt liberated as his lips claimed mine. I breathed heavily, my heartbeats racing, blood in swift flow, electrified skin tingling. He raised himself from his launched position, his bulge evident.

I let out a surprised gasp as he nibbled my chest. He grinned at the sound that escaped me, pausing to kiss me, his lips sloppy and wet as they went down on their business from my lips to my neck and down to my belly, each touch deliberate and deepening. I let out a pleasurable moan as he went further down. I craned my neck to one side, gripped the bedsheet with one hand, the other lodged in his hair, playing with it, while he sucked the depths of my being.

I moaned loudly, head flying back as Dhruv let out a low hum, his eyes staring. He smiled, and his tongue once again started exploring every part of my body, and my lips bumped against my throbbing skin. I bit my lips to suppress a groan as his lips hungrily stroked me. His dark eyes wore a mendacious look. He popped open the lid of the bottle, smeared the lubricant over his fingers and brushed over the curves of my ass before moving inwards. Deeper and deeper. His hips raised reflexively, puckering with anticipation.

He gently pushed his finger inside me, as I breathed deeper, almost wincing. My hands fisted in the bedsheets. I let out a soft moan as his fingers moved deeper. His other hand brushed against my cheeks, his thumb fiddling with my lips, now pressed against each other. His finger gave a relaxing sensation, before his second finger also moved in. A mixture of pain and pleasure overwhelmed me as his fingers moved in and out of me. I lived the moments in short breaths. The anxious Dhruv had turned into a sensuous Dhruv. I gasped as a familiar feeling shot through my eyes. They were wanting and overpowered by his inviting looks.

Next, I heard the crinkle of a condom wrapper. The buzzing in my ears heightened. I gripped the bedsheet with one arm, and the other flew to his arms, digging into his taut flesh. Tears sprang in my eyes as he thrust himself into me, his panting breaths hot in my ears as his torso lay against mine. I let out a long, breathy moan as he softened inside of me. He collapsed on me, my arms wrapped around his back, his dark hair tantalisingly tickling my face.

The two of us lay there a while, catching up on our laboured breaths. I wore a victorious smile on my face. I rolled to pinion my body to his and rest my face on his chest. I pulled the sheet over our bodies. The sheets were warm with our love, and the warmth in him had rekindled.

***

"It almost seemed that you were possessed by some love demon," I blabbered, getting up from the bed.

"That's a tired analogy, hope you know that," he chuckled. "All I hope is that the demon that had possessed me was easy on you and didn't hurt you," he said amusedly, eyes crinkling as he smiled. I smiled in return as I made my way to the kitchen.

"Nope, it didn't. It pleased me," I chuckled. "Are you also feeling famished? I feel some good snacks will do."

He laughed heartily at my suggestion. "There's always food on your mind," he snorted.

I did some creative attempts at snacks—a winterish vibe, cosy concept. I converted a pair of buns into a pair of edible 'slip-ons' with scrumptious olive filling and grated boiled tofu toppings. It looked fresh and good.

"You clearly have a lot of time and heart to feed me." His smile widened, a few wrinkles forming at the corners of his eyes.

"Heart is a much stronger element here." I smiled my pleasure, my voice like some light, airy chime.

"What about I cook something for you…I would love that change," he said, mouth full; my eyes brightened with the thought.

"Last time you made me some salad and toast—a weird combination. But it was quite adorable to see you do that. And if you wish to put some effort, then I'd rather suggest we cook together." I chuckled.

"I never said I am great at cooking, I barely managed myself with ready-to-make options, and then there was always a subsidised canteen around. You are different; quite a maestro with pans and knives."

"Perks of being a little free, and in a long-distance relationship. I developed this love when things weren't good in my last relationship. Coping up is important. One needs to know how to find a channel to let one's anxieties out."

He listened to me intently as I spoke, expressing myself in short sentences, without building on any narrative. He seemed to steel his nerves as he let out a heavy breath, before his eyes met mine. He was getting the hidden meaning of my words.

"Maybe you are right," he said, almost fidgeting on the couch, his words choppy.

I looked at him, tense. I had to tell him, but it was difficult gathering the courage to tell him. "I have to make a confession," I said. He looked at him, a little unsure.

"Please try to listen to me. And don't argue about it. Just know that I did it to protect you," I added, almost as unsure as he was. Then, taking a deep breath, I said it in one go. "I told your mom about your childhood incident." His mouth immediately closed as he registered what I had said. "Please don't get mad at me for this. I thought she needed to know. She holds herself guilty of many things. And more than her, I wanted to know everything." I spoke and stopped. I waited for his reaction. He just stood there, emotionless. "I know it's your truth, and I shouldn't have overstepped, but I was just too full of rage to think anything. Please forgive me!!" I pleaded.

For a moment, silence hung between us—thick, unspoken, and heavy with everything we weren't saying.

"I don't know how to process this. But I'm not angry with you. She needed to know—and I know I could never have been the one to tell her. Even now, even after it's all out, I know we'll never really talk about it." He said softly. I could comprehend that inhibition.

"I know, when we talk about it, it seems that the entire past is replayed before me. It's incomprehensible. You know what people say about this 'living in the now' thing; that has always remained mumbo-jumbo for me. I know a part of me is just stuck in my past. There's no such thing as the present, it is just random interpretations of the past," he said, his voice gruff and deep.

"You are not mad at what I did?"

"No, Anu, I am just unable to process it."

"Then don't overthink. You deserved to know. It's about you. All I can say is that we are here to look out for you. Your mother may seem cold, bowed down by her own guilt, but she adores you and cares for you." I looked up at him, through my dark eyelashes, a hopeful, consoling half smile stretched on my face.

"I know that, Anu. But you know…"

"I know this. Just give yourself time. And don't think much," I reassured.

I tilted my head, smiled, and said, "We should do something to make this already perfect Sunday even better."

"That sounds good to me. What should we do – go out on a date?" he said in a suggestive tone.

"We can do that. Or if you feel too tired, I can make us something nice for dinner." I said, inching leisurely towards him and giving him a smile, which he returned earnestly.

"Do you genuinely love cooking—or do you just love cooking for me?"

"I take you as a good reason to pursue my love for cooking," I responded as I gently snaked my arms around his waist. He looked at me, and in the next instant, pulled me back, planting his lips over mine. When we parted, he smiled shyly at me in bliss.

"Let's order something from outside today. You sit here with me. Get some wine, let's talk…there's so much we need to catch up on."

I was glad that the agony and despair I had sensed in him had dissipated. I smiled, hoping he'd let go of his burden one day. What a flight he would take as a human being then, refreshed, anew, lightened of the weight of an unwanted truth; changed, and eager to embrace the change.

The Trail Begins

I walked into Melissa's office that day. I was pleased that I almost enjoyed unrestricted access to a cabin of a business tycoon. She was knee-deep in work when I arrived. Her eyes widened, and a salubrious smile stretched on her face seeing me. A genuine expression.

Her cabin mirrored her entrepreneurial spirit. On the walls were vibrant, eye-catching artworks giving a thoughtful appeal to the space, on the sides were swagged out couches and Ottoman chairs adding to the uniqueness and style, and the brightly laid accent table in the centre doubled up as a great conversation starter. I looked around to capture the appeal of her cabin. The main office was equally lavish and spacious, giving the entire area a contemporary and liberal look. There were pops of bold colours everywhere, and inspiring, eclectic furniture.

She signalled me to sit on one of the Ottoman chairs on the side and called for two cups of coffee. The appeal of her office was so different from that of ours. I realised something in her style; her style was more like mine than Dhruv's.

"How was Dhruv yesterday? He looked relaxed when he returned."

"The day went well. We chatted for quite a long time, and he was engrossed and equally engaged, unlike last week when he attempted more at making a pretence of being a part of the conversation. I told him that I have told you…" That caught her attention. But she looked composed – I guessed that's her usual stance – take things slow.

The coffee had come by then. Taking her first sip, she looked at me and asked, "How did he react after knowing that I know everything?"

"Quite composed. You should be content that he doesn't hold you responsible for anything. His discontent with you is more episodic than perpetual, and I guess it's more about his own insecurity. I even feel that he has forgiven that lady. He isn't someone who can keep malaise in their heart," I said softly.

"You're right, he can't. He is the kind of guy who would forgive everyone and punish himself. This extreme earnestness becomes painful after a time." Her mouth pulled slightly downwards as she looked at me. Our eyes met, and there was a hint of trepidation in her eyes. Mine remained hopeful.

I nodded. I took another sip and a bite of cookies.

"I have made the necessary calls to seek as much information about Dephny as possible. It's been over fourteen years. So, we might face issues tracing her. This is for sure that she has left Darjeeling. Her social media accounts are active, so that is some hope. The police are on it, and they assured me that they should be able to trace her down soon. We will have all the information then." She took a pause and then continued – "What do you plan to do after that, however, is the big question, and I wish to leave that decision to you."

"Face her to start with…I want to know who she is, her past, her present, everything. I want to see her behind bars," I answered in a definite tone.

She leaned forward and whispered, "I can easily get her incarcerated."

I swallowed thickly. A little scared, a little pleased. "Can you?" I asked, giving her an odd look and a reluctant smile.

"Yes, I can, and I will. She ruined my boy's life. She must face it." Her face was straight, no emotions, no frown of rage, no wrinkle of anxiety.

I nodded. She was right. And till the time she was out, she was a danger. A predator on the prowl. She looked at me with heavy eyes, and I could see the fears lodged deep in the waters of her eyes. Deep, I could see it was a hidden persona of hers, something unseen and incomprehensible. She looked at me with guilt set in her eyes, the sort of feeling that wanted to escape the dungeons of her eyes with the waters, a gentle, serene flow arising from the crevices of her eyes, washing down her balmy cheeks as some absolution, washing her of her undeclared sins.

We kept looking at each other, like two lost souls—losses moulded as flesh, brought together by a common tragedy. In normal circumstances, we couldn't have come this close. Melissa Shankar would have remained *the* Melissa Shankar for me.

"What are you thinking of doing?" I asked in a low tone.

"Nothing illegal, don't worry," she breathed. "I have asked the authorities there to get me every detail of this lady. Let's know her more, then we will see how to deal with her."

"Like using your influence…" I was confused and, in shades, scared. I looked at her eyes, the deep, piercing look like Dhruv's, but much expressionless.

"Influence exists to deal with these situations," she asserted, her face straight, voice deep, eyes unable to hide the vices.

***

We drifted from one topic to the other as we talked our hearts out. A smile on Dhruv's face meant life to me. I had no inkling I could love him so much in such a short span of time. He folded his hands across his chest and gave me a smug smile. I looked into his eyes. There was no trace of concern. The jovial him was back.

"I went to your mom's office, just to say 'hi' and offer some goodies," I said.

"And what did you two talk about?" He asked, bumping his head against mine.

"You know how much she talks, and how she talks." I grinned shyly, hinting at both her reticence and bluntness in tone. He gave a low laugh. "Well, she showed me some of your old pics, the kiddo, you, to the sweet sixteen, you. And what a bid collection she has. I must say, in your teenage years, you looked like a character drawn straight out of a romantic novel, an instant nut…and you were sort of cute as a child too," I teased, drawing myself closer to him, putting my hands on his sides affectionately.

"And what about now, when I am ready to step into mid-age," he whispered.

"Ahh! Somewhat tolerable," I chuckled.

Dhruv chuckled at my statement, snapping me out of my daze. I don't think he expected his mother to have those photos. Clearing my throat, I frowned as I peered up at him, who had started rubbing lazy circles with his thumb at the back of my neck.

"It was good to go through those, or learn about some of your childhood stuff, and then her own journey. She loves you; you know, she just could never express that, which is disappointing," I said softly, shaking my head. He listened intently.

"I know she does. I wouldn't have taken you to her if she didn't. I guess this inability to express love and concern for each other is mutual," he answered, voice heavy and full of regret, his hands clasping my head.

"Your relationship with your mother is beyond my understanding. But I appreciate the fact that she is supportive, at least you can do is to not be this cold with her. Either you or she, someone must break the ice. And honestly, seeing her, I feel you can do that job better," I said and waited to gauge his reaction. "Well, same goes for her, she can be a little warm too—to her son at least," I added in a sing-song tone. His smile faltered, his fingers stopped circling my waist, and a speckle of guilt arose from somewhere I couldn't pinpoint. Dhruv averted his gaze first, then, pressing his face against my chest, he hugged me tightly. I gently rested my head on his, and running my fingers through his hair, I asked, "What happened?"

"Nothing…I don't know Anu, but I don't think it's as simple as you think. This unappreciation has been normalised in us. We have lived like this for years. Not that we don't care for each other, but we are a massive failure in expressing our emotions for each other. And now you know why."

He blinked, his gaze drifting away from me before he continued, his voice quieter.

"She gave me everything I needed – whether I asked for it or not. But somehow that never built the bond I craved for. I have respect and appreciation for her. Anyone would. but I miss the emotional connection a son should feel for his mother," Dhruv paused, his words weighed down with something heavier now. "I am still trying to make sense of it. I have asked myself this question several times, but the truth is - I have not been able to forgive her for not being there when I needed her most." A string of tension hung in his voice.

"Just try that – try it for me…" I murmured. I had no idea why I chose those words, maybe because, that morning, I had glimpsed a mother's love he had never been able to see. I had seen regret in her eyes, and a will to do anything for her son.

He gazed at me for a while. I smiled and kept looking at his so-perfect face, letting my eyes declare my umpteen happiness I get from him being around me. After a caring look was shared, we found it impossible to suppress the incredulous, syrupy smiles on our faces. "Did you like her office?" Dhruv asked, a little out of context, but thankfully that nutty question distracted me from my mood.

"I loved it. I love her style. Now I know where you get all that charm from," I teased.

"Charm…" His large, dark brown eyes narrowed themselves in my direction, piercing deep into mine.

"Tell me more about what you guys talked," he asked. Ahh! So unromantic.

"Just normal, simple stuff—but I loved talking with her. And her enthusiasm for her venture is laudable," I was searching for right words to sell my lies.

"I would like you to meet my other family members and friends too. I sincerely feel like making our relation public," he said softly, leaving me both glad and surprised in equal measure.

"You really want to do that? Isn't it a bit early?" I asked, sounding confused.

"Only if you are willing to do that. I have been wondering about this for some days now," he mumbled, rolling his eyes, sounding a little apologetic for his eagerness.

"Babe, I am out of the closet, it's you who has to think of the consequences—your extended family, friends and even the company staff, you need to be willing and prepared to open up to everyone," I added.

"I can start easy - with my friends and cousins for sure. And for rest, I think it's time people get to know that. I can't hide it forever," he said, his hands rubbing up and down my arms in comforting strokes.

"As I said, I have no problem. You know I'll always support you in this. But I just feel that a genteel person like you needs a grand coming out," I chuckled, wrapping my left arm around his shoulders.

"I too had a party on my mind," he murmured quietly, and pressed a kiss on the top of my head.

"Our kind of a party, not the boorish straight parties. The vibes need to reflect the feeling of freedom of coming out. No stress! You leave that to me, I will plan that for you," I chirped enthusiastically. He gave me a soft smile as he leaned forward to rub his nose against my cheeks. "So possibly, you will be one of the handful of gay business leaders. That sounds quite a privilege – and inspiring too," I added.

Seeing my reaction, Dhruv kissed the top of my head and murmured against it, "My happiness lies in your happiness."

Some words are so simple, and yet your whole world can condense in those.

As I held him close and rested my head on his shoulder, every touch seemed to quiet the world—an unspoken plea to pause, to simply breathe in a moment where everything—our emotions, our thoughts, even the very purpose of our existence—felt distilled into something pure. In that stillness, it was as if all our feelings had condensed into a single, luminous memory—one where we lived solely for each other, not for anyone else.

In those six words, I found my world—a world I had grown so oblivious of. And there we were, cocooned, laying bare the honesty of our relationship in our eyes, and carrying the warmth and intensity of promises made to each other.

***

The next few days were different. Melissa remained fixated on Dephny and I looked like a spectator watching an old rivalry brim. But Melissa was a power hard to be contained, and she had taken on herself to trace Dephny. As I learnt, she followed up with her links in the police department, who had been able to trace her. It wasn't a difficult task considering our vast social media footprints. She had asked me to come and see her in her office, and I willingly obliged. I had also developed a fascination for her.

Keeping our conversations hidden from Dhruv and not dropping a hint had proven an arduous task. His love had made me so malleable to hide something from him. And he, with utmost ease, could see through my gestures—the narrowing eyes, the frowns, the shyness in my smiles, the tremble in my lips whenever he asked me of my conversations with his mother. My overly animate gestures to distract topics, and unnecessary expressions of love to avoid further discussions, had given him enough hint of what his mother and I were engaged in.

I increasingly scheduled my visit to Melissa's office for a time before or after my office began. That proved a respite from thinking of a lie or an excuse to Dhruv. Having your boyfriend in the same office is an unsaid limitation on your independence. You feel watched every moment.

I reached her office with a sinking heart. Rubbing my tired eyes, I pushed open her office door. She sat on her chair, studying a document. She looked at me, her face expressionless; a salubrious smile shared, and back to the document. I placed myself comfortably on one of the seats on the side. After some minutes, she turned towards me, with another smile, and walked to join me.

"I am sorry. I was looking at the designs developed for the cover page," she said, a satisfactory smile adorning her face.

"It's fine, you don't have to apologise for working." I smiled.

"What excuse have you given Dhruv to sneak out of office?" She chuckled. I laughed at that, nodding appreciatively.

"I adjust my office timings according to the time of my shows. I am now used to going around noon and then continuing a little longer in the evening. " I said, voice tranquil. "But before we start talking about other things, I wanted to tell you that your son has suggested making our relationship public, at least to a closed group to start with. I thought I should tell you; I wasn't sure if he would. And I feel you need to know this," I blurted, a little perplexed, trying to predict her reaction or a possible change in her stance from the pacified her to the pondering her.

She let out a hearty laugh, leaving me a little surprised, but more relaxed. Relaxing into her seat, she smiled at me and said, "What objection could I have with that? It's his life. He should decide for himself. But you," she added with a knowing look, "You surely are having a roller-coaster sort of life. So much is happening all at once. I wonder how you manage that."

Sometimes, even I wondered that. I smirked.

"I thought you hinted at giving each other more time before taking it to some conclusive end. Though I told him that if he wishes to make our relationship public, that will mean settling for something more permanent. I don't want to hop from one relation to the other," I stressed, my face scrunching up at the memory.

"The way you two understand and complement each other, trust me, this early is not early. I am happy for Dhruv, and as far as I have known him, he isn't a guy to choose a relationship to cling onto for some time and then hop to another. So, relax," she said, her voice genteel and relaxed.

"I am glad to learn your approval of our relationship. Dhruv is indeed lucky to have such an understanding and progressive mother," I murmured, my eyelashes flushing with faux innocence.

"What about your family?" It was probably the first time she'd asked me something personal. And I had no answer. I had long since taught myself how to live without their approval.

"What about them?" I responded, taking a huge amount of air in. Her eyes bore into mine. "I don't know what to say. My sister approves of the relationship, and she is the only one who matters. She will tell my mother now, and my mother, though still unsure, will convey her regards in some way. She won't accept me with open arms until my father approves, which I don't think is ever going to happen."

She listened to me intently, then tilted her head to the side, and said, "I may never be able to take your parents' place, but count me among people who will always stand by your side. You are a son to me." She placed her hands on mine. I could only wonder and grow appreciative of that endearing gesture. I chose not to say anything, nor did I had the right set of words to voice my feelings. I only smiled.

"Thanks for saying that. These small gestures mean a lot," I said in a courtly fashion.

He Asked Me

"Anuj," Dhruv said, leaning in close as his voice dropped to a mere whisper.

"Yes?" I breathed back in kind, vision a little glossy as Dhruv kissed the other corner of my mouth, lips lingering, partly satisfied.

"May I ask you something?" He asked, pulling me closer, arms wrapped around my neck, eyes teasing. I nodded.

"Will you marry me and spend your life with me?" That was dense, really, really dense. I had expected something like that from him—maybe even always wanted it—but nothing could have prepared me for the moment it actually came. I had no words, I choked, and Dhruv chuckled as he kissed me square on the lips. I hummed in satisfaction.

"You know my answer," I wailed, burying my face in his chest, as he laughed, running his fingers through my hair. What I truly longed for was that moment—-the one where my prince would slip a ring onto my finger. Or maybe that moment was still waiting for me.

"Should I take that as a yes?" He asked again, softer than before.

"Yes, idiot, yesssss. I'll love to spend all my life with you," I replied, cheeks flaming from emotional exertion. He smiled a soft smile and clasped my face. I felt a flutter rise along my cheeks, the kind of feeling you could fold your whole life into—wrapped in an irrepressible smile. Who could have made me feel so complete? And all he needed was—one sentence.

"You know, gay marriages are still illegal in India," I chuckled, breathing against his chest. Ohh, stupid me…

"Who needs a certificate? Our love is our certificate; a legal stamp on it means nothing. And if you want a certificate, we can just shift somewhere out and marry…. Our engagement means living together forever and committing to each other's happiness," he said, rolling his eyes and putting up a lazy smile.

"I know. I get this." I mumbled.

My hands were entangled with his and body wrapped around each other in a holy embrace. I was able to feel his chest rising and falling steadily, and heartbeat pulsing through his shirt into mine. The feeling was magical. In that instant, a single sentence changed the world around me, and with every sentence that followed I felt myself drawing closer to the fulfillment of my deepest emotional desires. I felt complete resting my head against his chest, listening to his comforting words and dreaming of a future with him.

Seeing his pleased reaction, I grew more embarrassed, wiggling out of his arms. He didn't stop me, his eyes watched me happily. I looked at him from the sides, my eyes asking him to continue. "How would you want this to go? Any thoughts on that?"

"Seriously…you told me you want to do this; then shouldn't you be the one planning it?" I drawled teasingly, leaning back on one side.

"Then you leave it to me entirely." He smiled at me, fiddling with my hair. "And I think it's even better if I don't plan much, just announce it and see how many of them turn up."

***

Goaded by endurance, I reached out and grabbed him by his shoulders. "I don't know if it's right or the best thing to do," I said, my warm words against his mouth.

"Me neither. But a part of me wonders—why not? Why keep hiding? And what exactly are we hiding anyway—our love? The most precious thing we give each other." He stood completely still. My face had gone pale, my eyes wide as I looked up at him, caught between disbelief and something deeper.

He gave me an intense gaze, as if trying to measure the depth of my consciousness. And then his lips curved in an involuntary smile, which expressed less of zeal and more of concern. "You know just chuck the deciding part, or the thinking part. I want to do it, I always desired to do this, and that's all that should matter." he said affirmative.

"Yes sir, I understand. Let's do it. Fuck the world!!" I answered in equal measure. A part of me believed in the crack of light I could see and had an inkling to advance in that direction; the other part still scared to take that plunge.

"Yes, we don't have to unnecessarily put up with this." Saying that, he tightened his arms possessively around me. He looked at me and kissed my forehead. "Let's only think about the future, our future. And the future is not in holding the truth back, but in being brazen about it. If people talk about it, then we will let them have their share of gossip, but it's we who must be true to ourselves," he said in a reassuring tone.

I bit my lips. Despite my guarded independence, I knew I depended on Dhruv's quiet strength. Probably he was right. Everything had happened so suddenly, it felt unreal—like I was still catching up with the moment.

What a big deal time is! I have been a sorry bit of time myself, a tiny container to pour stories in. Stories had kept getting poured in and out of this container, my entire life, and I had adjusted myself to live my destiny between these pourings.

"I can't think of a happier moment than being seen as your life partner," I said softly, my voice weighed down with emotion as I clasped his hand. "It's just… something in me keeps urging caution." I had this uncanny habit of being both stubborn and unsure – often at the same time. And no one had endured that contradiction more than he.

"Don't worry. Just take time to think about it. We will have an engagement when both of us are ready," he said, concern melting at his unguarded, half-opened lips.

***

Sitting on the floor by the couch, legs crammed beneath the smooth glass surface of the coffee table, I let out a fatigued sigh. The last few days had been a little too much to take. Pulling my glasses off to rub the bridge of my nose, which had started aching, I closed my eyes to rest them for a moment. I stretched my weary limbs. Dhruv had asked me for an engagement, Melissa was happy, and I was a little cautious, but willing. Everything seemed so different.

I went to meet my mother to tell her about the engagement plan and, to my surprise, instead of the usual 'convey my regards,' she said, 'I'll come to bless you both.'

The unspoken agony of years melted in one sentence. I somehow managed to hold back my tears, but when she opened her arms for a hug, I broke down into a flurry of tears. My heart swelled. My emotions were finding their way out. My father displayed no feelings. I knew that moment that our relationship had turned irreparable.

The response from my mother, said and unsaid, was heart-warming. In her welcoming smiles, all the indifference, fears, and pains contained within our hearts and caught in the depths of our eyes, washed away. I hugged my mother and cried. For a gay man, a hug of acceptance is life-changing. It's like growing out of our shells, where we live conditioned and withdrawn.

Melissa had been a pillar of support in this. I could get that from Dhruv. His appreciation was visible. Her concern for him was evident. She was a lioness guarding her cub, fierce in her love—but the wounds of the past had carved a chasm between them, sometimes too wide, too deep to cross. Still, they were trying.

Dhruv had planned to call for a gathering of our close friends and family. More than a coming out session, it was to recognise our relationship. Dhruv was, no doubt, enthused. He had his elaborate plans for the day. I was mostly abiding by his plans, not wanting to be a party-pooper. I had no idea how those seven days were to go. Dhruv had insisted on keeping everything secret from me.

How, I thought, even coming out for us gays is such an occasion. It's like a ceasefire after a civil war. And my war ran for almost a decade; his even more. Even before I knew the word 'gay', I knew I was different. And long before I could even name that difference, the feeling had already taken hold—I had no control over it. I wanted to know why I felt different, but I didn't have the means to explore. Or the reasons. Or any idea. There was no start or end to that - it was like a long, dark tunnel, or a never-ending, tempestuous sea.

I grew up alone, hiding myself, protecting myself from the numerous judgmental stares, the name-calling, stereotyping, and those unforgivable homophobic slurs which reduced me to an identity, a shape, and a face which stood out owing to its difference. I could never be who I was, and I could never escape. Growing up, I realised how individuals are reduced to definitions. If you don't play sports, you laugh loudly, dress differently, you don't fit in the accepted norms of a 'male', and so you become incomprehensible to the world. And this world doesn't like enigmas, it loves definitions.

I was constantly checking myself, worried that my actions might make people around me uncomfortable without meaning to. The responsibility was always on me; I could wrong an individual or a group because of my actions or just my mere existence. The reverse was unthinkable. I was always the different thing that never fit. I realize now that waiting for others to validate my identity was a mistake I made. I craved constant validation from them to feel pretty, smart, successful, and, above all, a normal human like others.

After coming to college, I realised how friendships and associations give you validation. Insensitivity and hatred toward identity often evolve, over time, into ignorance and indifference toward basic rights. You stop mattering to the people around you. And as they prepare themselves for a life with a job and security, good money, holidays, fine dining, parties, fancy exhibitions, movies, and salary increments, you and your identity become more and more invisible to them.

And then you realise that your identity is distilled into a three-letter word, and this three-letter word becomes more precious to you than all your professional or personal attributes. You try to find more of such three-lettered people, and you live your life with them. You cover yourself, find a shelter or escape, but you survive this internal war. Some take less time, some more—but everyone fights this war.

It took just two sentences to draw me out of my oyster, to help me make peace with my life, and to let go of the past, giving me the chance to see life with fresh eyes. The first came from Dhruv when he asked me to settle down together, and the second from my mother as she came out of the shadow of my father to support me in my decision.

Where's My Wedding Suit

As I swung open the white picket fence and let myself into the lobby, I heard the unmistakable clicking of cameras. They were there for Melissa, circling her like a group of young, highly groomed Sunday shoppers. She looked at me and, ignoring the cameras, walked towards me with a beatific smile set on her face. That was a smile of accomplishment, or perhaps great pride.

"Prepare yourself for this, being the first openly gay couple in the media fraternity, you two will easily become the topic of interest."

Honestly, I was left flushed by her words, first with embarrassment, followed quickly by annoyance. "I don't think that will happen," I huffed, following her to a table on the patio.

"Seriously, feast your eyes. I see a lot of circles breaking with this engagement. And well, before that happens, you need a fashion consultant. Imagine big, son. We're keeping it a private affair, but in an industry driven by events and headlines, it's hard to keep things truly close and personal. We all need to be seen striking the right chords. And to that, I have asked my team to draft LGBTQ-friendly policies for the company. I shouldn't be seen as a person striking the chords, but with her roots missing."

"I don't know much about image makeovers, but I won't mind getting some. Dhruv dresses so elegantly, and I look like a chaff with him," I moped, much to her amusement.

"Enough of this ugly duckling complex. Given a fair chance, you could easily make it into the official list of the adorable lots," she hit back. "A little makeover will take you notches higher than that."

My heartbeat was beating fast. It was how 'going crazy' feels. Not because of what Melissa said to flatter me or convince herself to accept me as her son-in-law, but that it was happening, and I wasn't in some elves' land where everything you desire comes true. It was the same harsh world I had always abhorred for othering me and reducing me to my sexual identity. And then that moment, everything seemed to have whizzed away, a life I had lived looked faded and withered, and a future stood before me where I could see a lover, a family, and hordes of people for whom my sexual identity didn't matter. It was just a crazy, nice feeling, something you can never prepare yourself for.

"Lost again in some thinking? Both of you share this trait."

"Nothing. I still feel I need to keep pinching myself to believe this is becoming a reality," I replied, dabbing my eyes.

"Pure hearts like yours deserve unimaginable happiness. I am happy for you both." I smiled at her courtesy.

"I wish that happiness for you, too. I want you and Dhruv to resolve everything." Maybe that wasn't the right time to say that. I should have started believing that time would heal all wounds.

Her expression changed, her blushing face narrowed, and then, managing a smile, she said, "You know, as brightening as the word 'love' may be, it casts long shadows. I agree, I might be using this to repair what's broken between me and Dhruv, but as a parent, I feel I should always be there to support my kid, whatever my beliefs or values are. I wasn't there then, but this time I want to be with him. Maybe that's how we would be able to thaw things between us."

"And I will be happy if things get better between you and Dhruv. And I feel it quite has, haven't you noticed the change?"

"No, it won't happen till the time he feels the vacuum that episode left in his life. That's how old wounds are, even after they have healed, the scar remains to remind us of those sordid times."

I hummed in agreement. She guided me past some photographers. "On a different note, maybe I can get you two covered in my magazine," she breathed. I inhaled deeply and reminded myself to stay calm. I smiled to brush off the conversation. I was sure Dhruv would object to that, and as for me, ah, I had no qualms, but for her, it would be too much of patronising herself.

She smiled casually and handed me a glass of Pellegrino. Rich tastes. Sometimes, her tastes and choices made me feel like I wasn't meant for that family. But then there was Dhruv—an icon of humility—who showed me that life could be lived in simple words: no pretenses, no patronization, just raw feelings and a heart that yearned for truth.

***

We took one big step in telling the office colleagues about us. They were aware of my sexuality, but Dhruv's came as a surprise, a raw shock to some, and a handful, a delightful insight. Some had contemplated seeing our closeness, easy judgements that are passed off as verdicts, only to be validated with time. It was a difficult part for me, but then the truth had to be told. And at times, truth leaves you brimming with happiness, like that one.

The reactions of some of my colleagues did more than bring tears to my eyes. There was true happiness, but beneath many smiles lingered a trace of sympathy, a quiet awkwardness in their gentleness, a discomfort with the status quo, and a subtle contempt for conformity. Their warm hug came wrapped in appreciation for my temerity for braving this world order and battling my way out. They wouldn't have cried for someone else, but their tears did drop for me. And from their tears, I could sense how narrow our worlds were, where every step of ours towards the guided and preached normalcy would be treated as a win. How had we come to carve this situation, this order, where different worlds exist for different people?

Every little feat is glorified. Acceptance and appreciation bring tears. And the very normal and sacred truths of life, like marriage and family, become stories that need to be told to inspire an entire generation. No, we weren't symbols to be patronised. We hadn't performed a heroic act—we simply loved and dared to dream of living that love. It wasn't an act of defiance or a battle won. And yet it was something worth celebrating, something that could be woven into a song of destiny, sung to awaken hope in wandering souls.

"What are you wondering? Come along, there's so much to be done," she cried, and I raced to catch up with her. I wish I could tell her what I was wondering. Everything was so quick and unpredictable. A month ago, I was oscillating between Dhruv's dark past and our uncertain future, and then an evening conversation changed the course of my life. I had begun to cherish every moment—even the ordinary had started to feel like a rare indulgence, something to savour like an unexpected luxury.

And I felt this change around me. I looked down from my balcony at the park below—a stretch of green broken only by puddles of water, where people walked or cycled each morning and evening—and felt a quiet contentment settle in. I noticed and relished the distinct wintery shadows on the trees cast by the Sun. I walked the same diminutive stretches of road and felt an unseen, yet perceptible change. The same stretches I once despised now carried a fresh whiff of change. Even the dull walls revealed hidden hues. Everything around me felt brighter, renewed.

"You are as excited about the engagement as Dhruv is. I seem to be left behind in this by miles," I said, getting close to her.

"Excitement is in our genes. I am sure you have your way. Now skip that and tell me, what colour do you like?"

"For what?"

"For the dress you'd want to wear on your engagement evening. I have got exclusive rights to choose the best outfit for you both, and one of my designer friends is all set. It will be casual and obviously regal. Gone are the days when you could show up in an OTT sherwani and get away with it. You two will be watched by all, and you need something to carry that class," she announced.

"I hope you are not writing a wedding speech, and googling 'wedding toast jokes' to crack that day!"

"Well, that's in the list too," she chuckled. "See, this is going to be a formal event, where we are announcing the coming together of you, and so we can surely afford to have the environment a little light. Wedding jokes won't ruin the matter." She looked at me, waiting for a response, but I don't think I had any choice except to agree with her. And before I could say a word, she went on. "And as for the dress, I had some thoughts. I was thinking you two could experiment with some silhouettes for the evening, and we could do a nice photoshoot in some timeless wedding trousseau a day before the event. I can get those arrangements done."

"I have no thoughts on this. Seems like I am still processing that this is happening. I never had an inkling I'd see a day like this. The wedding was something beyond even my dreams."

"Well, pinch yourself to come to reality. It's happening. This is destiny's way of being nice to nice people, so that people don't lose hope. Ask me; I have lost so much of my child's life that I wish to be a part of every second of his life now…" she said in a heavy voice.

"Please, not every second, let us have our moments too," I said jokingly. Her eyes crinkled as she smiled.

I smiled back, a quiet realization blooming in my heart—a realisation of being set free, finally allowed to live what was due to me, every moment, every notion, every idea, every pause, and the mysteries that lay beyond them. In many ways, Dhruv and I had lived parallel lives —his tinted with shadows, mine with the unknown. We had walked bloodied paths, wandered through untraced tracts, and weathered the season of fall in our hearts. And now, here we were, ready to walk down the aisle—not just as lovers, but as partners.

***

"Your mother is way too excited about our engagement," I said, taking a sip of my fully caffeinated coffee; the decaf with Melissa had drained me of my usual energy.

"I can get that; she messaged me seven times yesterday, reminding me of different unrelated stuff. And that's her usual routine from the day I told her I'm going to ask you for an engagement."

"Ah, and you didn't tell me that," I said, narrowing my eyes.

"Well, I knew you would tell her that anyway," he chuckled. "This overzealousness has now become normal for me. I took almost a week to find the opportune moment to ask you, so that way it's been almost three weeks since I have been seeing her this enthused. At times, this chirpiness amazes me, and at others it just grows on me. Wish I had half her level of energy."

"Forget that. You need to explain me if devouring the last night's leftovers was the most opportune time you could think of to ask me for engagement; great timing, my boy." I blushed, my cheeks red with ebullience.

"Because it's a difficult thing to say, no matter how much you love the other person. I have realised there is no opportune time to tell someone you love and that your life is incomplete without them."

At that moment, I could think of no better gesture than a hug to express my feelings. A mixture of expressions flickered through my eyes. I swore under my breath to fill his life with all the brightness I could.

The fan above our head whirled lazily, casting lines of moonlight against the ceiling. The room was quiet, with only the sound of his breaths audible to my ears. While everything within the walls remained calm, a storm of emotions raged quietly inside us. But we held that storm gently between us, and little by little, we filled it with love.

"We should go on a holiday after our engagement," he said, suddenly.

I looked at him and smiled, a cherishing smile. He had stolen my words. I wanted that too, to slip out of our chaotic world and spend some time together. Just us, spending time to know each other better, and exploring a different world together.

"The idea of a vacation is always inviting, I'm always game for it," I said, my eyes widening with passion.

"And we definitely deserve it. And where do you want to go?" He asked, rubbing his nose against mine.

"Let's start with Istanbul and go on a cultural and culinary expedition."

"Start with…" he snorted, arms hugging me tighter as he rested his head in the crook of my neck, muffling his laughter, "and for how many months are we thinking to take this vacation?"

"Let's plan for three months, and then we can think about extending it." I chuckled.

"Sounds like a plan. Anyway, no one will miss us. You make the plan then," he said, giving me a mischievous grin.

"Yeah, no one will miss us, except for the office where you are the strategy director, your mother, who is on an ever-extending business expansion plan and wishes to rekindle the old mother-son bond, and my elder sister, whose serotonin level goes down if she doesn't see me for some days. I'm sure I won't miss anyone," I said, narrowing my eyes a little and sliding my hands up to wrap them around Dhruv's neck.

"All I do in the office is take calls, which I can do from wherever we are. My mother will miss me for some days, but will understand, and probably this may strengthen our bond. And for your sister – if she misses you a lot, then probably she can join us there for some days, at least this way I will get to know her better," he said, leaning closer, his chuckle making his lips tickle mine.

"No problem! If my director's kind enough to grant me that many days off, why should I complain?" I said, teasingly, tilting my head with a playful smile.

"Ahh! Now there comes the office protocol thing. Now I will need to rethink this plan," he said slowly, dropping his gaze from my eyes to my lips pointedly, making my stomach flip. I swallowed, preparing myself for whatever game he was conjuring in his mind.

He looked deep into my eyes, his hands tugged on my hair, and we engaged in a soft kiss. On disengaging, he whispered in my ears, 'love you always'. I rested my head on his shoulder and clung tightly. I whispered back, 'Always.'

The Unhealed Wound

"You can hate me for that, but it's only you who can do it," Melissa said in a tone more serious than her usual self. I sat there with an unfamiliar unease. My sister had joined us for the conversation, and she sat with her brow furrowing in deep concern.

"Taking it back to him is like pushing him down the hole again to assuage our egos," I said gently, fiddling with my shirt in discomfort.

Melissa's steely face managed to soften a fraction, "Anuj," she said, a small sigh leaving her lips, "we only had two options when we started: justice and forgiveness. And we agreed that both these options are exclusive. Forgiveness is not justice. I believe only you can break this news to Dhruv and convince him to do what he must. I'm leaving it entirely to you to decide when, or even if, it needs to be done. But the longer we wait, the harder it might become."

"And, not just as a mother but as a human being with genuine concern for others, I want Dhruv to speak up. No matter what the consequences. It might hurt him, but it is a necessary thing to do," she added, giving me a long look, her face twitched as she seemed to try to find the right words. I turned to my sister, who looked grave and in complete concurrence with Melissa. She nodded to me, her eyes looking down apologetically.

"If I am to do this, I would want it done before our engagement. I don't want to carry that burden for long."

"Cautious Anuj, what if something untoward happens?" My sister sighed.

"I know the risks. If that means calling off the engagement, then we will call it off," I breathed with unease and impatience.

"That's inevitable," she said with an admirable evenness. Her look focused gradually, and her eyes took on a metallic gleam. "I hope you don't feel unnecessarily obliged," she added flatly. My body felt like clay with the mere thought of stalling our engagement. Though unsure initially, I had gotten quite used to the idea of settling down with someone I love and us being recognised as partners. I didn't want anything to ruin it—not even the truth Dhruv deserved to know, or the responsibility he was meant to carry.

"No, I don't," I said squarely. "I'll do it," I added, breaking my tone and submitting to her request, stating each syllable separately, and then looked into her eyes. Her eyes were clouded with mystery.

My sister squeezed my shoulder to express her support. Melissa remained unmoved. At times, it felt her want of revenge from Dephny overpowered all the gentleness and love she had.

"I will ask him to open up and shelve that burden of truth off him. Things need to be told," I added, a hint of doubt evident on my face.

I was scared at the thought of asking Dhruv to open up and share the secret he had kept with himself for years. Maybe what we thought was silence was his closure and reconciliation with the horrid past. It was difficult for any of us to predict how Dhruv would take the matter. We had to be ready for the worst and be there for him. I could picture myself cocooning him in a blissful embrace of silence as he battled his past. The weird silences are usually the scariest of things. I was preparing myself for that.

***

My occasional defiance wasn't enough to deter her. Changes in my body were visible, but the turmoil in my mind remained hidden. I was battling with something more than the constant abuse. That was far deeper and far more perilous. I didn't just hate her; I hated her kind. I was failing to find trust in an entire kind. I was turning into a mental monolith of steady mood and no excessive emotions. I knew then it would take years of hiding to come to terms with mental and emotional normalcy.

There were feelings I was failing to understand, attraction for some getting dwarfed by contempt and remorse for others. The indifference was growing in me, like a malignant tumour, killing off my emotional cells and producing an indelible bias. And then I realised that the tale of my fight to exist was evolving into a tale of my life and love. My struggle was not just limited to coming out of that situation; I struggled to be able to hold reins of my life.

I was failing to figure myself out, and there was one I could turn to and talk to. I called my mother, for that seemed the only plausible way out of the cold mess I was in. Sometimes, I would wrestle with who to blame more—my mother, for never asking about my troubles or checking on my well-being, or myself, for continually failing to share everything with her. Was I too afraid of everything, or had I grown stolid, the abuse normalised and taken as a part of life, or was it that I had lost all hope that my mother would help me? Interestingly, I had known her too little to make that judgment.

But that day I called her, and all I could do was cry on the phone. I didn't utter a word. She kept asking, and I kept crying. My mother listened to my sobs; her concerned voice changed from shaky to remorseful. She was understanding me or making a genuine attempt to do so. Then I realised that all I had to do to stop everything that had been happening to me was to make a call to her and talk. And that took me two years. Two long years to cry and tell her that there was something wrong. I put the phone down and drowned in my sobs, my stomach knotting and my heart sinking.

That evening, my mother called my grandma and told her of her plans to take me back to Mumbai. She was concerned about me. That night was the last time I talked with my grandma.

I don't know what egged me more—my silence, my grandma's indifference, or my mother's undeterred belief that everything was fine. My call that day, and my grandma's sudden death the day after, brought my mother back to Darjeeling.

Her earlier visits had been more confined to the management of tea estates than to me. It would be wrong to say that I wasn't a part of those, but I was just a part of those. She used to come to see her estates and not her son. The estate would buzz with activity whenever my mother arrived—everyone on their toes, ready with their records and updated balance sheets, and my mother would meticulously go through them all. In every way, she was witty, observant, finicky, and exact—all she lacked was a little compassion. My mother was always a complicated person, difficult to gauge or predict for anyone. And all her complications did was push her away from her son.

My mother did not shed tears at Grandma's funeral. No, crying in public wasn't her thing; that was for weak souls. I wondered if she cried alone in her room. Her eyes looked bewildered and a bit scared. Time must have become a peculiar kind of mirror maze for her. Things seemingly close were far, and things far away were close to her. These mazes have a predictable habit of changing, from funny to frightening, without sounding much alarm.

Her eyes were aware of me; I could feel that. She might never have shown compassion the way you expect from a mother, but she was responsible, that I knew. Often, she would ask people around her abruptly— 'Is my son okay? Has he taken his meals? He was close to his grandma. Is he doing fine?' No, that wasn't right. I wasn't close to my grandma. She was indifferent to my presence in the bungalow, but then, how would I expect my mother to know her? She believed in what she was told, or what she thought was the truth. We never had those candid conversations that would have allowed us to truly know each other.

The bungalow was a tranquil place that Sunday. It didn't choke with humanity as on other days. The funeral was over, my mother had met half the town, had closed-door discussions with lawyers and industrialists, and conducted herself in all the religious ceremonies. She spared time to be with me, though we didn't talk much. There was nothing much to talk about. Perhaps we didn't know how to talk with one another.

The town wore a deserted look; the citizens must have decided to loll about till midday. The only hub of activity was an old bookstall run by the A.H. Wheeler. There, newsboys busily sorted out Sunday newspapers to cater to the hill city's news-hungry multitude. Later in the day, they could be seen hawking the Telegraph and The Statesman with other dailies.

My mother went late at night from my room. We had a long chat, something we had never had before. Hesitancy and uncertainty were the key characteristics of our chat, as we delved on various subjects from my falling school grades, the legal ownership of the estates going to my mother, her advertising firm close to achieving break-even, to her wrecked personal life after the tumultuous divorce episode with my dad and a legal battle that followed to get my custody. But in those long chats about her life, her business, and her career, my problems remained unattended. She never once asked me why I cried when I called her. She might have made her conclusions. On occasions, I tried to confront reticence, while my mother encouraged conversation. The flow might be lacking, but after a while, my shyness slackened and yielded, allowing some impression of the true personality to emerge.

"I got my tickets done after your call and have your tickets to Mumbai with me. I've kept you at a distance for far too long," she said softly.

The words rang in my ears. Probably she looked into my eyes and comprehended what I had wanted to say. Anything said then would have discouraged all further talk, and back then, I was decidedly curious and inordinately enthused to talk more. Perhaps that was my quest to know her more. And I was just relieved that she had come, and I had my tickets to Mumbai.

"We will leave shortly, once all the paperwork here is done. I understand I was wrong in sending you here, and I understand you felt lonely here. Just remember that I was equally pained to be away from you. I wish I had learnt this before," she added, taking me in her arms. I had seen so little of my mother's motherly gestures in life that every moment that night seemed worth living and clinging to.

***

As if on a cue, Dhruv came over and enveloped me in a bear hug from behind. He buried his face in my neck, planted some kisses, and said, "I hope you have some time for me; of late, you spend more time with Mom planning for the engagement."

I wriggled away but failed to hide my pleasure. He was right, of late, we had not been meeting regularly. I had taken a week-long break from work to make all preparations for the party, but more importantly, I was avoiding him, for meeting him would have meant taking him back to the past he had left behind. He took my hand and led me back to the couch. Sitting comfortably, he looked at me and solemnly asked, "Tell me how bad you are going to surprise me that day?"

"You should rather ask your mother about that, who is consistently adding on the guest list, menu, and every possible thing. Do you know, we are supposed to go for some designer clothes?" I answered, both in awe and surprise.

"I saw that coming when she asked me to stay out of it. She will decide for me and incorporate your opinions wherever she can. That's my mother, I know, deft, meticulous, and equally domineering."

"But I am just loving it. I had never expected that she'd be so open about our relationship. Did she always know about your sexuality?"

"I presume so. I earlier thought that she was overdoing it, for she is caught in a guilt-trap. I now realise it's just that her gentility and concern are often masked by her tough attitude. And then this time, her love for me has found a channel to come out."

I laughed a slow, sardonic laugh. I put my hands on his thigh and, taking my time to prepare myself, I asked, "I want you to do something."

"And you think I can say 'no' to you," he answered, smiling.

"The task is not that easy," I looked at him, my eyes serious, "you have to tell the Darjeeling police about Dephny and what she did to you. We learnt of other horrible things she has done, and there is no evidence to try her for any of the crimes. The police need a statement to start making all the enquiries."

"We," he remarked, and I looked at him like a miserable fool. He was determined to be shocked, and I had weighed all options and then sided with the truth. For a moment, we just looked into each other's eyes, and then he broke the uncanny silence set between us, "Don't look at me like that. I am not blaming you. I don't think we can understand each other on this. There's no need to try that even. Never mind. I guess the fault is mine, I kept this hidden from my mother, who could have saved me, from everyone else who could have sympathised with me, and to a great extent, even from myself. I was always holding it back. You are among the handful I talked with about that horrifying episode. And see all you did was bring it back to me. The episode that had made me hate myself and hate everyone around me. I wanted to forget that Anu..." His voice became coarse and heavy.

"Not when there are consequences—and not when it's not just about you. Your mother went to the police, asked them to dig deeper into her. Believe me, this goes far beyond you."

"That's my mother, Anuj, you know her. She is caught in a guilt trap, and that is egging her on for revenge. You can't trust her until you know things first-hand. She doesn't walk the line—she lives at the edges of good and evil," he said, his voice half-drowned in sobs.

"Then do it for yourself and face your apparitions. What she did to you was not just. And forgiveness is not always justice. And oblivion is never the answer. Or just do it for me...We don't want to continue our lives knowing there is always this mess, semantically and in all other ways. What is our life supposed to be for, when there's always a sulking feeling that we failed to stand for each other? Are we to spend the rest of our lives trying to identify each other, knowing there's always something that can draw you away from me and make you a recluse in your loneliness? It's not just about you, it's about us. I don't want myself to be in the same guilt trap your mother has been for years, and then keep telling myself 'Wish I had done something'. You answer me that..."

He remained silent for a minute and then nodded. He agreed to tell the Darjeeling police. That was his true coming out—not in words, but in the courage to face his greatest fear: his past. I looked at him and failed to control my tears. I was crying for him, and in those drops gleamed my hopes and his fears.

"Thanks, Dhruv," I whispered in his ear; a smile flashed upon his face as he hugged me tightly.

***

I don't know whose fight that was; I never cared to know. I was unsure if a simple statement against Dephny could provide Dhruv a quiet yet revolting burial of his past. For Melissa, it was never just about justice—it was revenge, dressed in the delicate guise of concern. For me, it was to put an end to an episode that had troubled our relationship. It was my closure. And even while Dhruv was giving his statement to the police so that they could investigate further, I wondered if that was the end or just another long pause before the ghosts would come back to haunt us? Was there ever a thing like starting over?

I could still see the traumatized teen in him, trapped in time, never allowed to grow past the pain. Healing is exceedingly important after a painful experience, and Dhruv had chosen to repress his emotions for so long before opening up to me. Healing had become practically impossible. But as Melissa had said, this needed to be put to a justifiable end. Dhruv could hide himself in a shell, but for us, living with that truth had become increasingly difficult. The shell needed to break.

It was difficult to gauge if Dhruv was relieved or simply keeping his emotions tightly sealed. That night, he slept like something wildly improbable—stripped of emotion, his body a vast, pulsating machine, its skeleton making subtle adjustments in the dark. Beneath that still surface, an ocean of emotions churned: the waters of its consciousness swarming with haunted anxieties, sudden flashes of intuitions, myriad undiscovered secrets, deepening needs, and swelling greed. All of it remained hidden, even from me. He needed his space, a constant of his, anchoring himself to his emotional isolation, like an eremite, unwilling to be touched.

The Wedding Bells

I laugh when I think about it now, but on the morning of my wedding, my heart pounded with nerves. I'd seen him in so many different moments, over so many years—but each time the thought struck me anew: we were about to exchange rings, to be wed, with our family and friends watching as two lives come together. Each time this realisation hit me, it stole my breath. I'd find myself pacing up and down my room, quickening breaths, as if motion could tame my nerves. I was nervous.

More than the idea of the wedding and the settings, Melissa's idea of giving the wedding a contemporary touch had made me go weak. There was some work going on in every corner. It was nowhere a casual affair; the preparations made it look an affair of epic proportions. Thankfully, Dhruv's allegiance to a versatile, ever-smart suit that flatters all proportions was undeterred, and we didn't have to oblige to her idea of draping a rusted blue blazer with a tailored *mundu.*

My sister came to meet me in the room. She wasn't alone; I was gaily surprised to see my mother standing there. She was smiling with her arms spread to take me in.

"I hope I can be forgiven," she whispered in a low tone.

"Hey, Mom, you don't have to, I understand everything," I replied, wiping a stray tear.

"I couldn't miss this day. Parents live to see their children happy." I hugged her.

"I can't tell you how happy I am," I whispered.

"Your father is not here, but I know one day even he will..." She couldn't complete the sentence. A drop of tear ran down her cheek.

"I understand. It's not him, it's his ego."

Outside on the lawns, Melissa had ensured resplendent arrangements. She had decided on a personalised installation in the middle of the bar, which included the hashtag #MadeForEachOther. There was an over-display of rainbow themes, our favourite songs played in the background, and much more. It was complemented with a tailor-made carpet, and our story ran on the screen in the centre of the lawn. Yes, I had sent her all our pics, and the designer in her gave them the everlasting script they so desired. And there were huge cut-outs of her, the Mad House advertising, and enough references to her to be launched lifestyle magazine.

She bubbled with joy as the screen shifted from one dreamy setting to the next. And I made sure we captured our moments—with wine, coffee, and even breakfasts—preserving the small details along the way. There was sleepy Dhruv, and then Dhruv in the kitchen, Dhruv in a business suit, in his tees.... actually it was mostly Dhruv, and less me. But it was Melissa, and I wasn't complaining.

She looked at me, and how she was trying to contain her feelings was just a treat. My mother and sister had taken a corner for themselves. I could feel Di feeling restrained with my mother in those settings. Melissa inched towards my mom and took her into the comfort of her arms. My mother was nervous, just like I was, but her anxiety carried a trace of guilt, and mine a sense of gay abandon. I looked at the future, and my mother looked to erasing the past.

From the window of my room, I could see the two mothers mingle, probably share a light joke, and laugh. On the other end, my friends shared jokes over cocktails, while around a table sat Dhruv's cousins, reliving their moments of reunion. There were some business colleagues of Melissa, some who's who of the advertising world, and then somewhere around the centre, happily settled with a glass of wine, calculated expressions more like a little estranged in a familiar world, were Dhruv's first boyfriend's parents. I couldn't hold a smile looking at them. Oh! How could I not love this guy who treated everyone with so much respect?

"Seems you will take more time to get ready?" I recognised the voice coming from the back. It was Aarya.

"Hey, bud, I am just looking at the gathering on the lawn. I am so full of emotions, Aarya. It's uncontrollable, and I am so nervous right now. I am literally getting goosebumps every ten minutes."

"Oh no, bestie, this anxiety is all over your face. Just absorb it. Live the moment. We are all so happy for you," he said, giving me comforting looks.

"I know, but still, you know. I mean, how do you prepare yourself mentally for something like this? I had never imagined this day for me. Even in my wildest dreams, I couldn't have thought of so many people assembled to celebrate for me, or just that I would get wed, I mean, exchange rings, and then vows, and then stand before so many people as a couple. It's overwhelming. Call it something beyond overwhelming, I don't have a word for that."

"All you need right now is a hug..."

Ah! Yes, I did need a hug to get myself together. And I hugged my best friend tight and took a deep breath. It seemed that the air that had been stuck was released, and as it was released, it comforted me, bringing me to a normal state.

"I hope I am not interrupting the bromance of two lovely friends," Dhruv said as he hugged me from behind. He looked flamboyant. His chestnut hair was swept back, just the way I liked it. The black suit and white shirt he wore fit him perfectly, covering his broad shoulders and his well-chiselled body.

I smiled, my heart feeling so comforted then.

"Well, we have two options — either we have a round of drinks here and then go down, or we go down and then have a round of drinks. I feel so nervous right now, I can feel an electric pulse running down my entire body, and I want to soothe that electric feeling. I desperately need a drink to relax, and then we can get dressed up and go down."

"So, there was always only one option?" I winked. He smiled back. There was never.

There was a certain lightness in the way he spoke. How proud I had always been of his humor, and how effortlessly I could read the honesty in his eyes.

"You two are getting that *pre-marital* stress, or whatever you call it," Aarya added.

"Didn't you and Dhriti get that?" Dhruv asked him as I got to prepare a round of drinks for us.

"Oh, I definitely did. From boyfriend to husband, that's a huge transition. I had developed cold feet,"

"Dhruv, he developed such cold feet that we had to postpone the wedding date." I teased, handing them their glasses of white rum.

We had a drink, followed by some hugs, some deep breaths, and then we came down—together—as a couple to the world. Aarya followed us, and Dhruv's cousin joined from his side. And we walked slowly, hand in hand, towards the podium. From afar, I could see Melissa with my mother. Next to them were my sister and Dhriti. My mother's eyes were heavy; Melissa's looked elated. She took my mother's hand in hers and they walked towards us. The spontaneity in everything around me was riveting. It's like everything had stopped, and was moving at the same time, more like an intersection where the future and past met.

"You can't imagine how delighted I am to see you two starting a new phase of life together, as life partners," Melissa said, her voice choking with joy.

My mother took my hand in hers, and before she could get her words to pour out the storm within her, I threw myself in her arms. The heaviness in her eyes was haunting. Years of guilt and regret weighed on her—years of staying away, trapped by boundaries that kept her from expressing the affection she longed to show her son, who needed a steady, uninterrupted flow. But that wasn't the day, nor the place.

"We need your blessings," I sighed briefly, looking at her.

"You know you have it. You always had it. You will always have it," she said, looking at me, while silent tears ran down her cheek.

"You have our love and blessings, and even though circumstances had been hard for your mom, I am certain her heart cried every day for you. Certain feelings don't need words," Melissa said.

"A request, mothers, before I start feeling anxious and he being him drowns himself seeing all the love around, can we share rings and then resume these conversations? The night is long, I assume," Dhruv said in a pleased tone.

"And before that, may I just do some formality?" Melissa interrupted

"I told you, Mom, no wedding speech. This is ridiculous, it's so 'putting you on the spot' irritating." Dhruv's frustration came out as a shy laugh.

"Who on earth said it's a speech. You know how much I hate to hog the limelight," Melissa answered, obviously containing her angst at being put down by Dhruv. We rolled our eyes at each other with that 'Oh really' look.

And the next moment, the soft music started. Our story as a colourful video flashed on the screen, and champagne was brought in. We looked at the honesty of the moment.

Ultimately, two people who love each other must ask themselves to commit to each other, releasing themselves of their freedom, and agreeing to the boundaries of a relationship. Marriage is like a fearful gamble; it is like putting a lot of things aside to see each other grow together. And then with each step, you realise love is not some possession, it is participation - it's realising what it takes to move together, coexisting in a little shell, where you see your ideas and beliefs merge. You grow together, and slowly—almost without noticing—you become someone entirely different.

But these ideas had always felt foreign to me—until Dhruv asked.

And there I was, happily entering those sacred boundaries. But deep in my heart, I knew I didn't crave for security or permanence; I wanted continuity and flow—the freedom to be who we are and shape each other into our moulds without losing our individualities. I looked at Dhruv and gave him a carnal smile.

Our mothers brought us the rings. Yes, the moment had come. In that little, lively space with people whom we loved, grew, or worked with, around us, we exchanged rings. And boom, came some fireworks. By then, Melissa's craziness at the party had started hitting us in a lively way. And when she came to raise the toast, her uncontrollable rapture made me feel how foolish I was to have never imagined this moment.

"My sons, here I raise a toast to your love. May your love be modern enough to survive the times, and old-fashioned enough to last forever." She raised a toast. I looked at my mother standing beside me and hugged her tightly.

Champagne was poured in glasses, cake was cut and served, the soft music changed to something more romantic, and then people greeted, congratulated, and hugged us. It was pouring love, and my eyes were wet. But it was an unbelievable joy that waited to trickle down from them.

I looked into Dhruv's eyes. I saw the man I love—and who loves me—silently approach and sit beside me, just to hold my hand. Amid the clinking of glasses, the ebb and flow of friends, the drinking, toasts, and smutty jokes, he looked at me with his youthful eyes, holding hopes and promises. I held his hand close to my chest, and there we were—just the two of us, content, happy in each other's presence, speaking little, perhaps not a word at all.

And then he poured more champagne in my glass and planted a light kiss on my forehead. I felt the intensity and permanence of our love in his smile. Our love that existed in many forms—baubles of stolen kisses, trunks of secret words, trinkets of hugs, breaths of said and unsaid feelings, and purity of our smiles.

Epilogue

Majestically astride between two continents, a mystical playground of historical and cultural marvels, a palimpsest of civilisations, wrapped in an eternal time freeze, the timeless Istanbul stands witness to our love. Dhruv wanted to travel to Istanbul together, and a place so drop-dead gorgeous was too much for me to resist. We have come to the Asitane Restaurant, renowned for recreating flavourful Ottoman Turkish dishes. Next on the list is exploring the rich architectural wealth of this land, which has passed on from the Greeks to the Romans to the Ottoman Empire. Both empires bequeathed Istanbul a wealth of superb buildings and incredible experiences for souls like us.

He leads me to the small table in the restaurant. A late hour for dinner, and most of the tables are empty. He pulls out my chair. I sit. He sits across from me. A waiter approaches and, without saying a word, pours us wine and leaves the bottle. A shy smile comes to my mouth. He looks at me like a voyeur looking into a secret world. He smiles back. We lock our eyes across the table, and everything around us fades away. We can feel each other, our feelings calm, gentle, controlled, and with a deep sense of longing.

He watches as I sip the wine, losing myself in the munificence of Istanbul. I smile, trying to hold my pleasure. Time stands still. Seems like an eternity to enjoy each other's company. He is lovingly watching me. I am loving being watched. Anyone can see the energy between us. It can be felt. It's something surreal.

"What do you want to do after going back to India?" He asks.

"I think I will take some days to get back to my old self. We have been out for almost a month now. And then gradually get back to my show, and then go through all the magazines that covered our story. It's time to get back to the old life we were living and do what we have been doing."

"You mean restarting your show…"

"Oh, definitely, I am waiting for that. I wish to see what more I can do," I answer, looking deep into his eyes.

He smiles, puts his hand on mine, and whispers, "Always with you".

"Did you spare a thought for Mom's offer of working with her in her advertising firm?" He asks after a brief silence.

"I did. I introduced Dhiriti to your mom on the engagement day. You know, Mad House is her dream thing. And as for me, I wanna take things slow. And give me more time. I think I am going to split my time between my show, some writing, and some titbits in advertising. Quite a free run for some time now. And then I'll decide where to put what, or what to prioritize," I reply. His eyes travel over me, taking me in, before settling on my face.

"Does that mean we will see us less?" he says in an unsettling tone.

"We live together, Dhruv. You will see me a lot, just not so much that you get bored of seeing me," I chuckle, and he can't resist smiling at my expression.

"I don't know what I want to do next. Just continue with my work or do something more. I do wish to do more on diversity training and corporate sensitisation programs. But not sure how – honestly, there's a lot on my mind. Maybe the first thing I do is put it all down, and make somewhat of a plan," He takes a deep breath and continues, "I wake up every morning and think, 'I need to hurry up and do something.' What do you say, how should I start?" He says in a deep tone. I put my hand on his hands and smiled.

"I am already feeling so proud hearing this from you. You should make your plan. And I am very sure we will figure out ways to execute that."

"Guess we both have a lot to do when we are back," I smile softly, look into his eyes, and say, "…and at every step, I will be there by you."

From outside, you can see in the hearts of people; they make you feel warm, some rare ones burn like sunrays, ablaze with the intensity of their passion, they are a sight to behold! Dhruv has always been that rare kind for me. Not many lovers get a chance to reflect on the evolution of their relationship, which can be achieved if the fires in their hearts were to merge. We know ours will create a giant maze, with an ability to shine over many lives, restore hopes, and fire ambitions. As I listen more to him, I try to understand what made him initiate this dialogue on the last evening in Istanbul, a day before we fly back to India. Probably he has been nursing this idea in his heart for long, maybe the settings, or that he has come to terms with the liberty that accompanies truth. Whatever it may be, Dhruv now carries a heart light enough for his own to bear. And I listen closely when he speaks—because in his words, I often find my own thoughts.

It seems that a long battle has come to an end. We're lucky to have good people by our side—those willing to see us for who we are and honor what we want. But the fight is never truly over...

Acknowledgements

I always felt like a changeling in my skin, shifting from one phase to the next, transforming from one form to another. As a child, I believed I lived in an enchanted world—perhaps even blessed with some hidden, eternal power. While other kids prayed for better marks in their exams, I wished for the ability to control the weather. The old pile of rocks wasn't just mysterious; it felt meaningful, as if holding secrets only I could decipher. Wandering through the tangled bramble of the woods, I searched for magical mushrooms, half-expecting to find the wise caterpillar from *Alice in Wonderland*, ready to counsel me. I waited for an owl to arrive with a life-altering letter, one that would open a doorway to a different fate, where being different wasn't strange or crazy, but something rare, something blessed.

I searched for echoes of stories, tracing their whispers through time. I lived my life through books—learning from their plots, losing myself in their narration, feeling their emotions, and turning their pages as if they were the pulse of my existence. I read not just for pleasure, but to distill life into its purest essence. Yet, I never realized that with every story I absorbed, a writer within me was quietly taking shape.

As I grew older and came to understand my true self—the sense of loss and displacement that had once shaped my enchanted world—a different kind of story began to resonate with me. And so began a journey that had been embarked upon countless times, yet never truly completed. This was the journey of writing a story. First came a page, then a chapter, and before I knew it, the first book had been written.

But stories don't end with a book; they continue to unfold every day—in the way you think, the way you act, and in the people you meet. They live on, shaping your perspectives and evolving with every interaction. The second book is a journey through these encounters, a narrative woven from countless conversations across different media. With each exchange, I realized how much more there is to learn—and how many stories remain untold.

This book is dedicated to them—to everyone from the queer community whom I have met, listened to, learned from, and shared moments with. It is a tribute to the relentless fight being waged in every corner, a fight to carve out safe spaces, to express oneself in a world that grows ever more conformist and majoritarian.

To each of you out there, battling in your way—through art, words, verses, tweets, or even by simply placing a stamp or a flag on your social media, or just by being there—you are the courage behind these words.

No queer story is complete without acknowledging the activists who have dedicated their lives to advocating for identity, inclusivity, and diversity. You have given voice to an entire generation. To name only a few would be unfair to the countless others who continue to fight in their ways. If people today can push the fight forward, even in the smallest of ways, it is because of your unwavering spirit and relentless pursuit of justice.

Thanks to my editors and the entire team at Om Books for their tireless efforts in shaping the final version of this book. Words may not be enough to capture the value of our discussions—the afterthoughts and reflections that shaped this final version.

A heartfelt thank you to Suhail Mathur and his team at The Book Bakers, my literary agent, for your invaluable ideas, edits, designs, marketing insights, and, most importantly, for representing my work to Om Books.

And lastly, thanks to my family members, teachers, and friends for the positive influence you all have had on my life and for lending your ears to my oft half-baked stories. Your deep 'hmms, 'ahhs, and 'nooo, don't do that'—trust me, it meant a lot.

Author's Note

The novel is set against the backdrop of the Supreme Court judgement of reading down Section 377 in September 2018. Ever since its passing, critics have always asserted one thing: the *law won't change anything if society doesn't accept it; change has to be brought from within the society.* And while that statement may seem conservative, it is partially correct. The society, and the forces that shape the society from media, arts, literature, to politics, have a role to play to play to destigmatizing same sex relations or sexual diversity.

Celebrating acceptance is not liberation; it is not even close to the fundamentals of liberty and equality. Though it is a step in the right direction to normalise and harmonise public discourse on sexuality and identity. With a historic judgement, Supreme Court has officially recognised queer people as legitimate citizens, making the long, hazy road to equality and inclusivity clear. But the law can only initiate, and not conclude, the removal of a stigma in a society.

Come every June, the pride month, a temporal space for the proud assertion of all things bright and wonderful and queer, is created. The once 'deviant' is loudly and proudly celebrated.

The members of the community come out of their closets to celebrate their identity, companies join the chorus, and pave the way to creating more inclusive workspaces. But despite this boisterous acceptance, rejection still trails the community as a shadow. And that runs deep down, some as silent stares and some as overt rejections and negations of their identity.

There's an elephant in the room that has still not been addressed (despite many efforts). And there are normal, healthy, creative people paying a heavy price for that. There are countries where individuals/people do not fit into their *heteronormative* mould. Within many open countries, many subconsciously or consciously *tolerant* individuals refuse to normalise it in the name of culture, religion, "naturalness," and tradition. And there's no one answer to it—sometimes, it's the larger construct of the society that fails the queer, and at times the policy adopted in and the political construct of the country.

India's stance on LGBT rights (at least from policy adopted) has been an encouraging one—despite India decriminalising homosexuality, India abstained from voting in favour of LGBTQ rights at the United Nations Human Rights Council on a resolution moved by Latin American states seeking to renew the mandate of independent expert on protection against violence and discrimination based on Sexual Orientation and Gender Identity (SOGI). On similar grounds, in March 2015, India had supported a Russian-drafted resolution that opposed benefits for same-sex partners of UN staff. Back at home, in December 2018, India passed the transgender rights act, which has been called by trans activists' 'murder of gender justice'.

Unfortunately, "othering" the queer folks is still a phenomenon, and Indian politics, media, arts or business hasn't pushed forth its best to normalise the discourse. To me, even this seemingly innocuous act of 'othering' is a feeling of alienation and queasiness. Why do queer folks have to open up, when it is completely normal for straight folks?

As I coursed through writing this novel, I interacted with many queer and learnt their issues. It's such a wide spectrum to even understand every nuance; all one can do is give a patient ear to the folks and try acknowledging the issues faced by them. And in every interaction, I learnt that every story I listened to is a tale of the future generation. Queer issues have to be normalised to the extent that children who identify as queer are not made to feel different. This is our responsibility to the coming generation. One should never underestimate a child's ability to carry shame. We need to make things normal, normalising people's choices, their ideas, and identities.

With queer folks, they rarely get to grow up as themselves but as a version of themselves as the society defines their beings. Some grow up out and proud, willing to voice their concerns and desires, living a life of candour, and some as versions of themselves that sacrifice authenticity to minimise humiliation and prejudice. But queer folks get to live their lives in bits, surrounded by more questions than answers. And a major part of life goes into finding answers to those questions; at times in actualising and appreciating one's sexuality, then in picking parts that are authentic to them. And this goes beyond just their selves, the larger issue remains the lack of support systems, the network of allies, and the politics and advocacy to delve on matters about queer lives.

This will go a long way; the change is slow. But as we wait for the slow change to become transformational, many expressions die or are put to death by the prevailing heteronormative character of the society. Sexuality has always played a central role in self-expression. Ideas die because of a dearth of a more nuanced exploration of gender and sexuality. While we build dialogue around gender and sexuality, we can work towards creating safer places and ally networks. It takes certain plasticity and participation to accept and support every individual around one.

In our educational spaces, workplaces, or our homes, we need to start fostering a culture of allyship, especially in corporate settings, through furthering nuanced dialogues, sensitisation and advocacy, and enabling policies. Look around at our public places or corporate settings, there's a lot we have to achieve, and we haven't even scratched the surface. The societal structures need to evolve to take the conversation forward. They all have a major role to perform to help a community and create a supportive environment. Feelings of not belonging are not only detrimental to an individual but have a cascading effect on the quality of our societies.